Curate of Wermigey

Wermigey; or The Weir Amid the Water

A Norfolk Legend by the Beginning of the Wars of the Roses

Curate of Wermigey

Wermigey; or The Weir Amid the Water
A Norfolk Legend by the Beginning of the Wars of the Roses

ISBN/EAN: 9783744777155

Printed in Europe, USA, Canada, Australia, Japan

Cover: Foto ©Andreas Hilbeck / pixelio.de

More available books at **www.hansebooks.com**

WERMIGEY;

OR THE

WEIR AMID THE WATER.

A NORFOLK LEGEND

OF THE BEGINNING OF

THE WARS OF THE ROSES.

BY THE

CURATE OF WERMIGEY.

———

Once, we were Princes, proud of Name and Blood ;
Now, Cattle graze where our brave Castle stood!

" Fuimus!—et ingens gloria fuit ! "—
Virgil

———

KING'S LYNN :
THEW AND SON, HIGH STREET.

1865.

DEDICATED

TO THE

OFFICERS AND SOLDIERS

OF

ELIOTT'S LIGHT HORSE,

THE

FIFTEENTH DRAGOONS,

OR

"KING'S HUSSARS,"

BY

AN OFFICER'S SON,

WHO

(BORN DURING THE PEACE OF AMIENS)

WAS

FROM CORUNNA TO WATERLOO,

(1808—1815)

A

CHILD OF THE REGIMENT.

ADVERTISEMENT.

The occasion of this book was as follows: On the "29th of May, 1863," a brother clergyman kindly inscribed the present writer's name in a newly printed volume of the "Historic Records" of his own parish; and further, acquainted him with a similar work, by another clergyman, on another parish. By each of these works, he was both surprised and pleased; and soon began to regret that he had no hope of obtaining materials requisite to illustrate his own too poorly conditioned churches and "deserted villages" of *Wormegay* and *Tottenhill*. One day, however, while enjoying a ramble, over hill and dale, by wood and water, about the moor land between Wormegay, Shouldham, and Pentney, in company with a very young relation, he began to indite a few of the first stanzas of the ensuing *Legendary Lament*, which afterwards so unexpectedly progressed, that, on the following "26th April, 1864," it was concluded; and, at the instance of *another* brother clergyman, it was committed to the press in *June*. It does not answer to the *models* set; it is of a *semi-poetic* character, and owes something to *imagination*. There are some inadvertent *errors* which need to be corrected; some *rhymes* and *metres* which transgress exactitude; some *omitted stanzas* which ought to be inserted; and *fact* matter which should be adduced; it is also defective in a certain *arrangement* which might be improved. Only a few copies, therefore, are now printed, for the purpose of obtaining the opinion of friends—whether or not, it be worth re-printing, with corrections and additions more explanatory of the times, places, persons, and circumstances to which it refers, but the expense of which could not be as yet incurred. The *ballad metre* has been objected to, as unsuited to *modern taste*; but it is submitted that this very ballad metre marks the productions of the age of which *this ballad* treats; and is most likely to attract the youthful, and the poor; for it is the same *Earl Percy* who is celebrated in the old Border song of *Chevy Chase*, and also in the *Hermit of Warkworth*, whose misfortunes involved those of the last "Bardolph"—*Lord Bardolph* of "Wermigey," now commemorated.

The author also thinks it needful to premise that, though his story is laid in days anterior to the Great Church Schism, and that he therefore affectionately accepts the Old Religion, yet he does not, on that account, endorse any of the fatal errors of the *Roman Heresy*, any more than he approves the multitudinous vagaries of modern *vulgar dissent*, or the anti-Christian and unconstitutional injustice which blots and blurs the *Church of England*, as by (much misnomered) "law" perverted.

Although a member and a minister of this last "straitest sect of our religion" (*Acts*, xxvi., 5), he can "call no man master upon earth" (*Matt.*, xxiii., 8),— pope, prelate, priest, or potentate, court, canon, council, convocation, congregation, or convention,—he utterly repudiates them all wherever they are self-convicted *ligatures* upon "the liberty wherewith Christ hath made us free" (*Galatians*, v., 1), and *poaching traps* on the Almighty's manor of the human soul, to snare and strangle unsophisticated Truth and Right (*Psalm* cxli., 10). Yet he both thinks and hopes to sympathize with "many brethren" (however classified) who are, or may be, CATHOLICS INDEED.—(See *Jeremiah*, xxi., 34; and *Isaiah*, xi., 9; and *Habakuk*, ii., 14.)

See the Corrigenda at the end.

INDEX OF CONTENTS.

SACRED TO THE MEMORY

OF

THOMAS, LORD BARDOLPH,

BARON OF WERMIGEY,

NORFOLK,

ONE OF THE ALLIES OF

OWEN GLENDOR, PRINCE OF WALES,

AND

SIR HENRY PERCY, *otherwise* LORD HENRY PERCY,

BUT COMMONLY CALLED

" HOTSPUR,"

WHO WAS KILLED AT THE BATTLE OF SHREWSBURY,

FIGHTING FOR THE RIGHTFUL

KING OF ENGLAND,

AGAINST THE USURPER, then "HENRY THE FOURTH,"

A.D. 1403,

LORD BARDOLPH BEING ALSO SLAIN,

BEHEADED AND QUARTERED IN THE SAME CAUSE,

AT THE BATTLE OF BRAMHAM MOOR,

YORKSHIRE,

TOGETHER WITH HOTSPUR'S FATHER,

HENRY PERCY, the 1st EARL OF NORTHUMBERLAND,

A.D. 1408.

OUTLINE OR PLAN

OF

ANCIENT WERMIGEY.

Part I.

Page 16.

Verse 48.

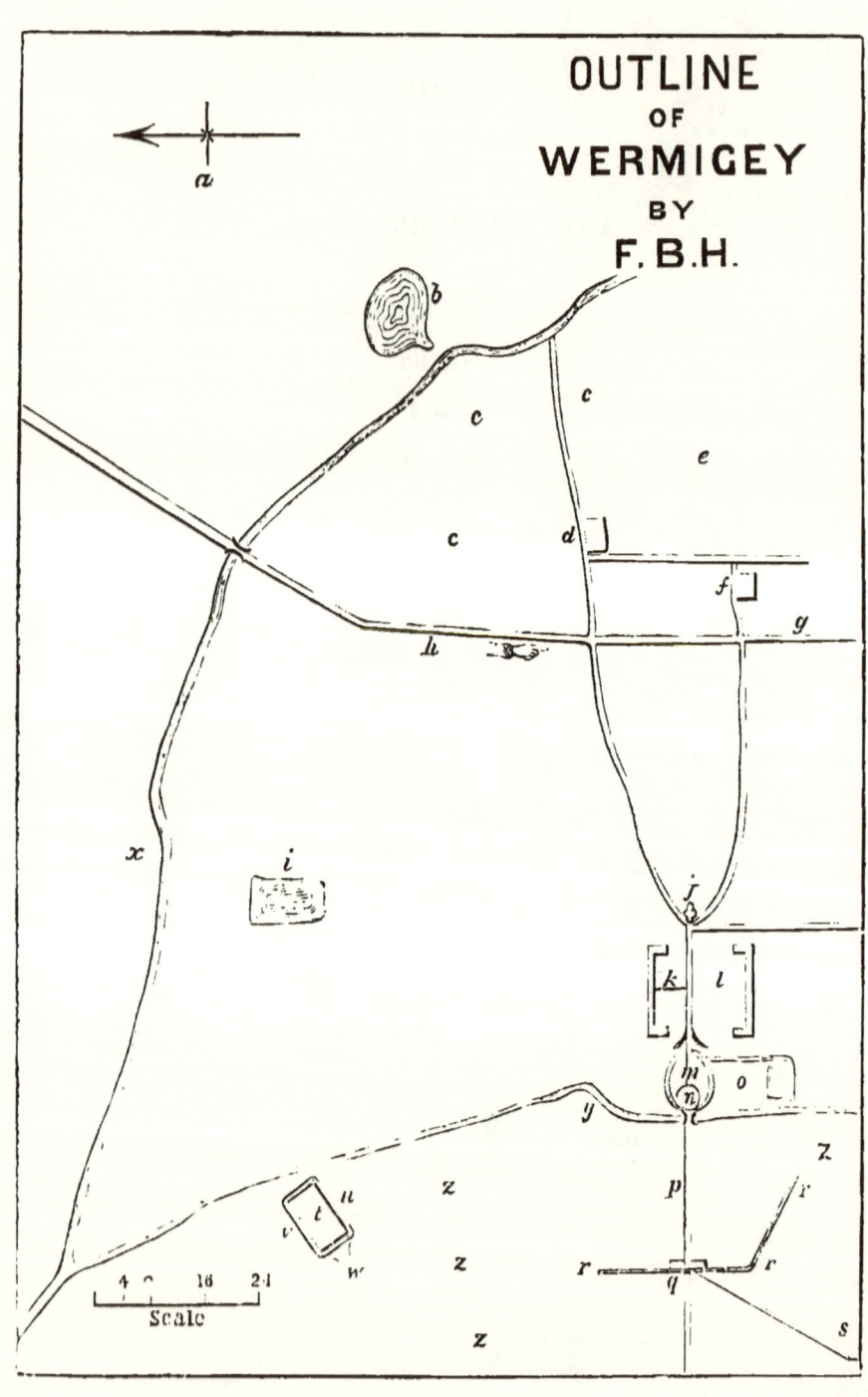

OUTLINE
OF
WERMIGEY
BY
F.B.H.

Explanations of the Outline, or Landmarks, of
Ancient Wermigey.

a. 1. The Points of the Compass.

b. 2. The New Decoy.

c. 3. The Wood—Park—Orchard.

d. 4. The Manor Hall, on the road to *Pentney* Abbey.

e. 5. The Goldings *(Godwins?)* Field of Bones, a Corner Head-
land.

f. 6. The Church.

g. 7. The Foundry Field.

h. 8. The Road from *Blackburgh* Nunnery to *Shouldham* Abbey.

i. 9. The Old Decoy.

j. 10. The Market Cross.

k. 11. The Guildhall.

l. 12. The Old Town Green.

m. 13. The Castle Close and Barbican.*

n. 14. The Keep, or Citadel.

o. 15. The Carousel, and Lake, or "Fish Pond Piece."

p. 16. The West Brig and West Brig Road.

q. 17. The West Brig Ward, *that is,* the Fore-Guard or Hill Guard.

r. 18. The Outer Fosse, or "Bully Dike."

s. 19. The Westbrig (now Tottenhill) Church.

t. 20. The Priory Isle and Close.

u. 21. The Priory Park, or "Bushy Field."

v. 22. The Priory Fish Ponds.

w. 23. The Priory Entrance—South West.

x. 24. The River Eye, or Nar.

y. 25. The Wermigey River, Sandy Drain, or Marham Water.

z. 26. The Lowland Fen, once under water.

— 27. The scale of 24 chains, each chain 22 yards, or ten chains
to a furlong.

* This is not quite correct, the wood engraver having blundered the
artist's design.

WERMIGEY.

PART I.

THE WEIR AMID THE WATER.

" Wermigey is environed with water, and low
grounds, fens, and marshes. The chief and most safe
entrance is by a causey, on the west side, where, on
the right hand, stood formerly a Castle. Here the
BARDOLPHS resided at times, being the head, or site
of the Barony of Wermigey."

" In this town was a Priory, founded by WILLIAM
DE WARRENNE (in the reign of Richard the First),
who died in the 11th of King John, dedicated to the
Virgin Mary, the *Holy Cross*, and *Saint John the
Evangelist*, for the Canons of *Saint Augustine*. No
remains of it are visible at this time. It was in a
close opposite the Castle of Wermigey, on the left
hand, as you enter the town; the Priory being on
the north, and the Castle on the south."—*See the
History of Norfolk, vol. VII., p.p.* 409, 502. *By the
Rev. Ch. Parkin, M.A., Rector of Oxburgh. Miller,
Albemarle Street, London.* 1807.

—0—

1.
Oh! the Weir amid the Water,
   I'll tell you where it lies :
In Western Norfolk, near Old Lynn,
   Five miles as the bird flies.

2.
Between two highways south and east,
   A desert looking spot,
Where Dame and Baron won'd to feast,
   Although now so remote.

3.
Oh! the Weir amid the Water
   Is where the sea-gull hies ;
Where the wild duck waits its slaughter
   And bustard sometime flies.

4.

Where the heron, snipe, and plover
Have room to range along,
And in free mid air to hover,
And sing their varied song.

5.

O'er wooded hill, o'er grassy plain,
O'er dike and reedy lake,
And streams which part to meet again,
And thus an island make.

6.

Oh! the Weir amid the Water
Is a *bank-land* of *Nar*,
Bounded by another water
That flows around so far.

7.

Oh! this Weir amid the Water
Is a *bank-land* of *Eye*,
For the name *Nar* follows after
The ancient name of *Eye*.

8.

So the Weir amid the Water
Means the *Weir*-in the *Eye*,
And in olden time they taught her
To be call'd *Weir*-ming-*Eye*.

9.

The *Eye* brink, *Eau* brink, *Eu*, or *E*.
Denote some *Water* by,
Which Biln-*eye*, Pentn-*eye*, Sedg-*eye* see,
As well as Weir-ming-eye.

10.

Weirmingeye was the centre of
An ancient Barony,
And the old suburbs, South, West, North,
Are so call'd to this day.

11.

The *Western* Bourg, or Berg, or *Brig*,
Call'd also Briggs and Bruge,
Is almost gone, but if you dig
There are foundations huge.

12.

Its church exists, but *Tottenhill*
Claims that old building now—
That once bare *hill* whose little *well*
Feeds the *Tot* stream below.

13.
Weirmingey—Wringey—*Wrungey*—too
People both speak and spell—
And so the two *Rung-towns* accrue,
The North and South as well.

14.
These villages that lie around
Have stories of their own ;
But none to match the *Water-bound*
For glory and renown.

15.
There was a spacious *Park* and *Wood*
Where still grow aged oaks ;
There was a *Manor House* that stood
Where now a Farm House looks.

16.
There was a well car'd *Duck-decoy*,
From whence a mile about,
No sportsman was allow'd the joy
To shoot a shot, or shout.

17.
There was a *Foundry* in the fields
For brass and iron works,
For helmets, battleaxes, shields,
Perchance for swords and dirks.

18.
There is a Field of dead men's bones
(God knows how they came there)
Of larger size than common ones,
As if pick'd men they were.

19.
Here may have been a battle fought,
And these the buried slain ;
Or else a church stood, now forgot,
And these all that remain.

20.
Castle, and church, and priory,
Canon and chevalier,
In a far gone antiquity
Did state and duty here.

21.
Here, in old England's early days,
When Saxon rulers reign'd,
Lord *Turkil* exercis'd his sway,
And warlike knights retain'd.

22.

Aye, many a tramp of horse's foot,
  With riders strong and tall,
Has cross'd that river-running moat,
  Beneath that castle wall.

23.

And many a cowl-clad monk and priest,
  From yonder priory,
Has gone to do *his* Chief's behest
  All round the Isle of Eye.

24.

And many a trumpet call and bell
  Has cheer'd the dead morass,
And summon'd over hill and dale
  To arms, and to the mass.

25.

Eight hundred years are past and gone,
  And even many more,
Since that old spot was fix'd upon
  To build a castle tower.

26.

Well chosen was the spot, I ween,
  For safety and defence ;
A *trigon* island each side in
  Two miles of water fence.

27.

The Castle on the brink of one
  Could deluge its own moat ;
And, though the foe might win the town,
  Could still be bravely fought.

28.

A round, uncorner'd rampart wall
  Girded four acres in,
And where the lofty Keep and Hall
  Were once, may still be seen.

29.

The eastward portal toward the Church
  Looked with a suppliant eye,
Though a mile distant you would search
  To see Heaven's Battery.

30.

Westward, behind the frowning keep,
  Over the river sluice,
The Drawbridge and Portcullis peep,
  For flight in fault of truce.

31.

Over the drawbridge, up the lea,
  A gently rising ground,
A *brig*, or bridgeway, you may see
  Through the low land around.

32.

This western brig, or west bridgeway,
  Thus led to the *west-brig* ward,
Where signals of alarm could say :
  " Arouse the castle guard ! "

33.

The outer castle-dike was there
  Cut through the higher ground,
Flank'd by the fen, whose waters were
  Another guarding bound.

34.

A bowshot from the battlements
  (Or a good quarter mile)
Would reach the line of that sunk fence
  With breast-work on the hill.

35.

Thence to the left, a bowshot more,
  The " West brig " church you mind,
And from its elevated tower
  A noble prospect find.

36.

The castle warder, he could see
  Both east and west church pile,
And, northward, the old Priory,
  On its own little isle.

37.

Outside the southern wall *façade*
  The knights off duty dwell ;
It was their favorite *promenade*,
  Their *place de carousel*.

38.

Here, a good band of bowmen could
  Severely gall a foe,
Coming along the West-Brig road,
  Through the West-Port to go.

39.

The water, and the breast-high bank,
  Nature's own fortalice,
Were worth three hundred (file and rank)
  In such a case as this.

40.

Part of the castle ground reserve
Was this select resort,
Within which was the Fish-Preserve,
The Baron's own choice sort.

41.

Outside the east gate's Barbican
Extended the parade ;
In later years, the *Old Town Green*
Before the *Guildhall* laid.

42.

The *Market Cross* the centre was
Of all the town and roads,
East of the Guildhall, and of course
The castle-guards' abodes.

43.

Thence, east-by-south, to church you come,
On the brow of a hill ;
And, east-by-north, the Manor Home,
Each road about a mile. .

44.

That comely hall, the manor house,
How pleasantly it stood,
Garden, and park with sheep and cows,
North sheltered by a wood.

45.

The Church, with solemn silence round,
Lay south a quarter mile ;
And in the east, the Fen beyond—
Old Pentney Abbey's pile.

46.

The *wood* lay towards one water way,
The straight stream of the Eye ;
The *church* o'erlook'd another sea ;
One pass'd the *castle* by.

47.

The wood, the church, the castle thus
Mark'd each side of the land,
Which now, like Canaan under curse,
Has lost its lord's command.

48.

Amid those waters of the waste,
With fish and fowl to spare,
Homes, church, and castle, all were plac'd,
In safety, and with care.

49.

Ah! Saxon men were stalwart then,
    And honest as their swords,
Ere Normandy's French trickeries
    Took truth away from words.

50.

Before the Norman Bastard came,
    With bandits in his train,
The power and property to claim
    Of free-born Englishmen—

51.

England's own Saxon Hengist bore
    The standard of our race ;
And brought the name, and fame, and love
    No other shall efface.*

52.

Invincible in honest
    Upon an hou
The traitor N
    Hopeless

Then

57.

In *Turkil's* time the day was theirs,
 Through dastard victory ;
And he, with many more compeers,
 Must abdicate, or die.

58.

The ruin'd Thane, defrauded thus
 Of feudal right and home,
Bequeath'd a patriotic curse,
 Which, in due time, has come.

59.

Of all those bandit Norman-French,
 Who took the style of lords,
And sat as Barons on the Bench,
 None now an heir records.

60.

The wheel of fortune has come round
 Since *Turkil* was a Thane :
The bandit French have given ground
 To Saxon and to Dane.

61.

Hermer de Ferrers reigned instead,
 First of the Norman lords,
And widely was his lordship spread,
 As history records.

62.

This *Shoe-smith* of the Norman horse
 The Bastard favor'd so,
To help him heel the Saxon force
 With many a kick and blow.

63.

Hence, both his name and war-device,
 Six horse shoes on a shield ;
Harmer the *Farrier* was not nice
 Who might be harm'd, or heel'd.

64.

Richard, the son of *Hermer*, he
 Sat on his father's throne ;
And by the style " de Wermigey,"
 An English peer was known.

65.

William, the son of *Richard*, died
 Without a male heir, then
His daughter *Alice* was the bride
 Of Reginald Warrenne.

66.

This Warrenne was a great-grandson
Of the fam'd Norman duke
Who, after Hastings' battle won,
The realm of England took.

67.

By Alice, Warrenne had a son,
William the Baron's name,
Who, ere he died, more laud had won
In Tottenhill to claim.

68.

This William paid, to free the King*
In Austrian fetters bound,
The sum of fourteen pounds sterling,
Part of the ransom found.

69.

He left one daughter *Beatrice*,
Who married *Bardolph Doun*,
And though this daughter married twice,
The heir was Bardolph's son.

70.

Hermer de Ferrers' blood-bought wealth,
And that of *de Warrenne*,
Thus, by the wedding of their stealth,
Became Saxon again.

71.

Bardolf's forefather, *Beard-the-Wolf*,
Like a true Englishman,
When the wild beast thought him to engulph,
He tore its jaw in twain.

72.

William Lord Bardolph, son and heir
Of six preceding chiefs,
Left also *William*, son and heir
To all his lands and fiefs.

73.

This William, in his father's life,
Took, as a gallant son,
De Gournai's daughter for a wife,
And still more wealth he won.

74.

Their son lord *Hugh* took Isabel,
The daughter of a peer ;
And for these two, God thought it well
A son Thomas to rear.

---

* Richard I., Cœur de Lion.

75.

On *Thomas Bardolph* (thus preferr'd
Tenth Lord of Wermigey)
Was, with the Prince of Wales, conferr'd
The Bath's Knight Heraldry.

76.

He married Agnes de Beauchamp,
A daughter of the lord
Of that same name ; and a son *John*
Was born as their reward.

77.

Elizabeth de Burg, his bride,
Grand-daughter of Earl Clare,
King Edward's cousin, and beside
Her own parents' co-heir.

78.

So that their noble heir and son
Was of the royal kin—
William, who held all they had won,
Now buried at King's Lynn.

79.

Take note of these four latest lords
Before we mention him
Who the chief interest affords
In *Wermigey's* sad dream.

80.

Lord *Hugh* was famous in the wars
Of Scotland and of France.
He aided the First Edward's cause
When order'd to advance.

81.

Lord *Thomas* was the special friend,
In knightly brotherhood,
Of the next king, who met his end
Through wanton womanhood.

82.

Lord *John*, he aggrandiz'd his name
By his wife's dignity ;
And favor'd by the Pope became,
Through their great piety.

83.

Lord *William*, with his father, oft
Would the Third Edward see,
When on return from *Rising's* Fort
He slept at Wermigey.

84.

Lord William, with that King's grandson,
    The luckless Richard, tried
In Scottish war to win renown
    The year before he died.

85.

William Lord Bardolph was the chief
    In wealth and in degree
Of all the Barons of the fief
    Of Castle-Wermigey.

86.

William Lord Bardolph was the last
    Who, at his death, could boast
Of all the honors he possess'd
    Not one of them was lost.

87.

William Lord Bardolph was the twelfth
    From the first Norman peer--
Would God! that, when he died, he'd left
    No hapless son and heir!

88.

As higher swells the mighty sea
    When nearer to its ebb—
As brighter shines the orb of day
    Over the glowing glebe—

89.

Only to reach the highest height
    To turn into decline ;
Such lot, as if decreed by fate,
    O Wermigey! was thine.

90.

Turn we to tell thy luckless tale,
    Thou desolate strong-hold,
And how misfortune could prevail
    Against thy Baron bold.

91.

William Lord Bardolph, Gloster, Clare,
    And eke "de Wermigey,"
Married his guardian's daughter fair,
    And children three had they.

92.

Lord Thomas one, to ruin doom'd
    Though fighting for the right,
Against a Rebel who presum'd
    To dare almighty might.

93.
Against a Traitor who dethron'd
His cousin and his king,
For the brief bliss of being crown'd,
Despite Remorse's sting.

94.
Against a Wretch who could devise
An agony extreme,
To slay the victim of his vice,
" The spectre of his dream."

95.
The Son of Gaunt indeed was grim,
Henry the Fourth his name ;
Richard the Second the victim
Of his dark deeds of shame.

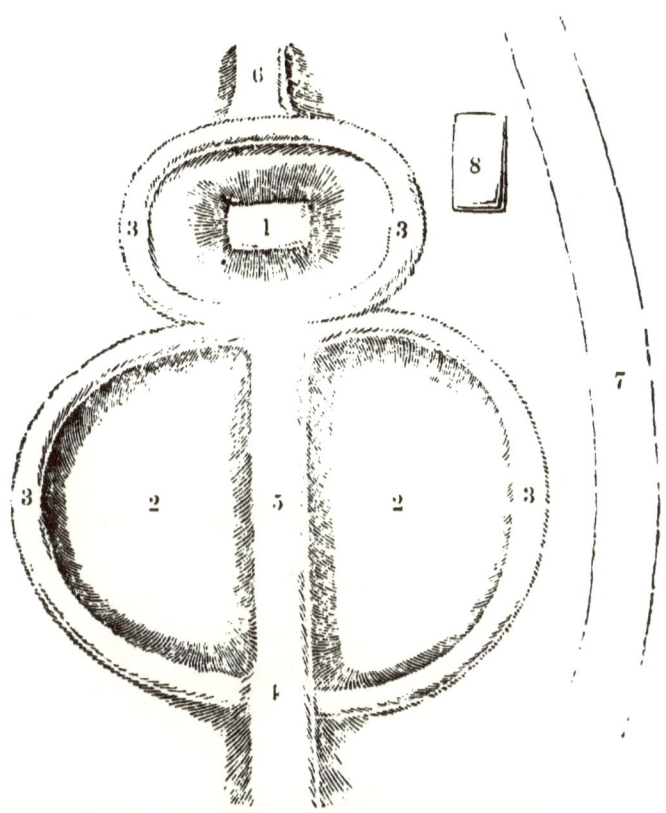

The annexed plan of the site and earthworks of the
ancient Castle of Wermigey was made on the spot,
in the year 1830; but it is by no means so correct as
it might be, in consequence, no doubt, of the artist
having sketched it from a wrong point of view, namely,
from the Eastern Entrance, which gives it the effect
of the figure 8, whereas, had the artist stood upon the
Keep Hill, and looked down, he would have seen that
the Fosse, and General Wall, were those of one GREAT
CIRCULAR FORT. The following explanation is con-
temporaneous with the sketch.

.. The site of the Keep, being a high mound, concealing no doubt the *débris* of the building.

2. 2. The Castle Close.

3. 3. 3. 3. Ditch with Bank Foundation of the ancient Rampart Wall, inclosing about four acres of land.

4. Remains of ancient entrance.

5. Remains of ancient causey.

6. Continuation of the same.

7. Modern road round, instead of ancient road through.

8. Farm House.

9. The ancient fish pond, only much further from the Castle than here represented.

For the loan of this plan, the author is indebted to the ever-ready liberality of Daniel Gurney, Esquire, of North Runcton Hall, near Lynn, as well as for the block prints of the arms or shields of Warren, Bardolph, and de Gournai, also annexed. See verses 65-69, 73.

The Shield of Warren.
Checquy, *Or* and *Azure*.

The shield of Bardolph.
Azure, three cinqfoils *Or*.

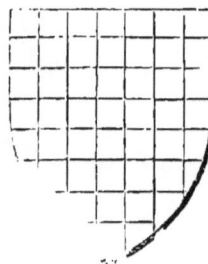

The varying shields of Gournai.
cross engrailed countercharged.

NOTE TO PART I., v. 59.

A comparative chronology of the Lords of Wermiger and the Kings of England during 470 years, by the respective dates of accession.

A. D.		A. D.	
	Harold.		Turchetil.
1066.	William I.	1066.	Hermer de Ferrers.
1087.	William II.	——.	Richard de Wermigey.
1100.	Henry I.	——.	William de Wermigey.
1135.	Stephen.	1169.	Alice=Reginald de Warrenne.
1155.	Henry II.	——.	William=Beatrice and Milicent.
1189.	Richard I.	1210.	Beatrice=Dodo Bardolph.
1199.	John.	1243.	William Bardolph=Nichola.
1216.	Henry III.	1276.	William Bardolph=Juliana de Gournai.
1272.	Edward I.	1289.	Hugh Bardolph=Isabella Aguillon.
1307.	Edward II.	1304.	Thomas Bardolph=Agnes de Beauchamp.
1327.	Edward III.	1330.	John Bardolph=Elizabeth de Burgh.
1377.	Richard II.	1363.	William Bardolph=Agnes Poynings.
1399.	Henry IV.	1385.	Thomas Bardolph=Avice Cromwell.
1413.	Henry V.	1407.	[Thomas Beaufort, Duke of Exeter].
1422.	Henry VI.	1427.	Joan Bardolph=Sir William Phelip.
1461.	Edward IV.	1441.	Elizabeth Phelip=John Viscount Beaumont.
1483.	Edward V.	1460.	William Viscount Beaumont=Elizabeth, daughter of Richard Lord Scrope.
1483.	Richard III.	——.	—Joan, daughter of Humphrey Duke of Buckingham, which second wife (widow) dying (after re-marrying) on the 16th June, 1537, this manor came to the crown.
1485.	Henry VII.		
1509.	Henry VIII.	1537.	Henry VIII., the great spoiler, when this ancient Barony was completely dismembered.

But, although William Viscount Beaumont died without issue, in 1509, yet, by his sister Joan, Lady Lovel, and her daughter Joan, Lady Stapleton, the blood of Bardolph is not quite extinct. In the year 1821, the author of " Wermigey," being then a youth, was acquainted with Sir George and Lady Throgmorton, the Poet Cowper's friends, at their then mansion at Weston Underwood, near Olney, Bucks., of whom Lady Throgmorton, " Catherina " Stapleton, was the daughter of *one* Thomas, and the first cousin of *another* Thomas Stapleton, the father of Miles Lord Beaumont, the latest representative of the ancient Lords Bardolph of Wermigey.

4

=Agnes, the wife of this Thomas Lord Bardolf, was the seventh daughter of Thomas Beauchamp, Earl of Warwick.

=Her eldest son, John Lord Bardolph, was born 13th January, 1312.

=And, after her husband's decease, on 15th February, 1323, (2 Edward III.,) she re-married Sir Walter de Cohesey, of Cohesey, Worcestershire.

=Her son, John Lord Bardolph, granted the parish church of St. Trinity, in Caistor, or Castor, (35 Edward III.,) to the Gilbertine Priory of Should-ham, for the better support of *Margaret* de Mont-fort, daughter of Thomas de Beauchamp, Earl of Warwick, *Catherine*, daughter of Guy de Warwick, and his own sister *Elizabeth*, nuns there; *Margaret* being the aunt, and *Catherine* the cousin-german of the grantor, John Lord Bardolph.—(See *de Legibus Antiquis Liber*, p. 186; also the *addenda*.)

WERMIGEY.

PART II.

MUTUAL AFFECTION, OR FIRST LOVE!

"As the Lily among the Thorns, so is my Love among the Daughters."
"As the Apple Tree among the Trees of the Wood, so is my Beloved among the Sons."
"Or ever I was aware, my Soul made me like the chariots of Amminadib."

Song of Solomon.

1.

Lord Thomas, when his father died,
  Was not yet seventeen ;
A youth of promise and of pride,
  Although his years were green.

2.

Frank-hearted, guileless, but quite clear
  In views of Right and Wrong—
Not doubting which he should revere
  With bias pure and strong.

3.

Afflicted by his father's loss,
  A melancholy shade
Grew with his young life's after growth
  And kept him always sad.

4.

Not, like some heirs, had he the greed
  Of being his own lord ;
He was not eager to succeed
  A father he ador'd.

5.

To him, his death was deadly blight,
  And made the world appear
A place of terror, not delight,
  Without his best friend near.

6.

Besides which, there are secret links
Between the minds of some ;
Such deep affection that it shrinks
Before the " world " to come.

7.

The " world " cannot appreciate
All that we understand ;
The springs on which our Peace is set
We keep in our own hand.

8.

Love, like Religion, cannot bear
Rudeness or mockery,
Therefore it is we so much fear
Vulgar publicity.

9.

And, though, of all loves, that between
A parent and a child,
The " world " itself reveres, when seen,
The " world " would have it chill'd.

10.

Too generous—too earnest—suits
Not sordid interests ;
And selfish jealousy promotes
Only its own behests.

11.

So let it do—and let it go—
We can afford to lose
The windy favor it may blow
Or not blow, as it choose.

12.

The youthful Baron did not spare
His knowledge to increase ;
He studied both the Art of War
And how to Rule in Peace.

13.

Dearly he lov'd his brother, and
Partook of all his sports ;
But often he alone would stand,
Absorb'd in his own thoughts.

14.

Long time, his widow'd mother view'd
And lov'd his sympathy ;
Until she deem'd it were not good
For youth too sad to be.

15.

The want of youth's *elastic* might
  In him, her spirit quail'd ;
To see *his* morning always night
  She secretly bewail'd.

16.

Mother and legal guardian both,
  Her own grief was at rest,
When this new cark—instead of sooth,
  Troubled her parent breast —

17.

As though she saw his future lurk
  Behind his cheerless brow !
But, when a woman sets to work.
  What cannot woman do ?

18.

" Surely," (she thought) " he may be brought
  By some new sympathy,
To take the interest he ought
  In the world's pageantry.

19.

" To feel some zest in his young breast
  Before he must depart,
To join, in death's eternal rest,
  The father of his heart.

20.

" Surely (she sighed) a fairy bride
  Might have the charming guile
To clear aside the clouds that hide
  The glory of his smile.

21.

" A youth whose tenderness can weep
  And so a *parent* mourn,
A fund as deep may also keep
  A wife's love to return.

22.

" Lord Cromwell's daughter *Arice-Ann*
  Is such a ray of light,
As might the dreariest soul of man
  Make sparkle with delight.

23.

" And, could they feel a mutual flame,
  (By God's most blessed will !)
Bardolph might not his mother blame,
  He might be happy still ? "

24.

So lady Agnes judged ; and so
    Lord Cromwell she advised,
And so they plotted for the two ;
    The plot itself disguis'd.

25.

In those days, marriages were made
    By parents for the young ;
And often these were happiest wed,
    And those not always wrong.

26.

Parental blessing was more sought
    Than that of the priesthood ;
Children, their children also brought
    To parents, as to God.

27.

The Patriarch Joseph brought his boys
    His own blessing to share ;
For children's children's children's joys
    He ask'd his father's prayer.

28.

So Lady Bardolph and the Lord
    Ralph Cromwell were agreed
Their aid their children to afford
    To make them blest indeed.

29.

Young Bardolph—Lady Avice-Ann,
    As if by accident,
But through an ingenious plan,
    Were to each other sent.

30.

They saw—they started—and they smil'd,
    As youthful lovers do ;
When each is yet almost a child,
    Bewilder'd at first view.

31.

Half-frighten'd, and inclin'd to flee,
    Yet wishing not to go ;
Half-curious (yet asham'd) to see
    What each might say, or do.

32.

They scann'd each other's form and face
    And features and complexion ;
They caught each other's innate grace,
    Each other's soul's expression.

33.
Each seem'd to each like a new *Dawn*
　Of Happiness and Health ;
A *Prospect*, infinitely drawn,
　A *Mine* of unknown Wealth !

34.
Each seem'd to each a *sacred thing*,
　A messenger of God,
Come to demand exchange of being
　Without a spoken word !

35.
Desire—dread—confusion—doubt—
　A new sense—a new life—
A something they could not make out
　Occasion'd inward strife.

36.
Timidly—tenderly—polite—
　All-generous at heart ;
So happy in each other's sight—
　So loth to have to part.

37.
As if unto each other chain'd
　In a lost liberty ;
Without the wish it were regain'd.
　Yet yearning to feel free.

38.
They looked and linger'd—for they know
　It must come to an end ;
Delighted beyond measure, though,
　The moments thus to spend.

39.
The sunlight—water—earth—air—sky
　All seem'd so sweet a view :
They never saw such scenery—
　Beauty and music too!

40.
As if reflecting bright ideas
　Chequer'd in their young breasts
With wishes, wonders, hopes, and fears,
　Day dreams, and night unrests.

41.
Like a swift voyage up the Rhine,
　A beautiful confusion,
In which Romance and Truth combine
　To realize illusion.

42.

A song of wordless melody —
A mute extravagance—
A waking to the verity
Of joys in abeyance.

43.

At length the maid, with maiden tact.
The silly silence broke ;
And, dealing simply with the fact,
Thus from the trance awoke.

44.

" Why look you so, fair brother ?   Speak !
If you have speech, confess—
Why are you thus so shy and meek ?
What means this strange distress ?

45.

" It seems I knew you long ago.
Though never seen before ;
Before we part, I wish to know
If you can tell me more ? "

46.

" Sister ! I know not what to say ! "
He gasp'd, with much ado.
" I wish to tear myself away- -
I wish to fly to you !

47.

" The moth around the candle flits --
The flower draws the bee—
The butterfly the sunshine greets—
And you have spell-bound me.

48.

" Fain would I worship, kneel, and weep,
Because—I know not why !
My pulsing heart I cannot keep
At rest while you are by.

49.

" You are too lovely, too divine
For mortal man to see ;
I feel asham'd that you should shine
On such an one as me.

50.

" Your speech is like an angel's song
Sweet melody your voice ;
My senses all to you belong ;
I have no will or choice.

51.

" Your vision stays me where I stand,
　To stir I have no power,
I long to take you by the hand,
　And die this very hour."

52.

The maiden sighed a plaintive sigh,
　Like a night wind's lament,
Or, as it were, a dove's death cry,
　Or song bird's anguishment.

53.

Humility so fair, so fond,
　So tender and so true,
To that she could not help respond,
　But "dying" would not do!

54.

The cloudlike sigh went fleeting by,
　As, with a sunny smile,
She whisper'd " You must never die!"
　And took his hand the while.

55.

" Your look proclaims how good you are,
　Your voice is like the thrush ;
And though too sweet for me to hear,
　I cannot bid you hush !

56.

" It is not me you mean to praise,
　But Him who made us all ;
Your words are like a poet's lays,
　Whose soul is musical.

57.

" The simplest beauty he adorns,
　Because he has the art ;
And you gild mine like a May morn's,
　All through your own kind heart.

58.

" The soaring lark, the nightingale,
　To warble are well known,
And you from them have learnt to *rail ?*
　In such a witching tone."

59.

" Sister!" he said. " in *raill'ry's* spite
　(Could I commit that fault)
You are as Lightning-in-the-Night !
　As Glory-in-a-Vault !*

* " The Angel of the Lord shined in the prison."—Acts XII., 7. &c.

60.

"More gladdening than the golden ore,
  More genial than the spring;
More generous than summer store,
  Or vintage gathering.

61.

"He who made you a morning ray
  Mine eyelids to unclose,
Made me to say my soul away
  In praise of what He does.

62.

"As flow'rs, refresh'd with heaven's dew.
  Breathe back their gratitude,
So my delight, derived through you,
  I utter as I should.

63.

"You, like that Awful Purity
  Which only saints behold,
Both fascinate the meek like me,
  And terrify the bold.

64.

"More 'terrible' to me, indeed,
  Than all I ever fear'd,
I fear thy loss—I feel thy need
  To love and be revered.*

65.

"The war steed, when he roams at large,
  We cannot help admire;
Yet who dare meet his mighty charge,
  Or face his frantic fire?†

66.

"So, sister! at thine eyes' sweet shrine
  I love to watch and pray;
But, when on mine thy glances shine,
  I shrink, and swoon away."‡

67.

He kiss'd her hand with 'bated breath,
  And then he let it fall—
As trembling on the verge of death—
  Electrified withal!

* "Who is she that shineth forth as the morning? fair as
the moon? clear as the sun? terrible as an army with banners?"—CANTICLES, VI., 4 and 10.
† "I have compared thee, O my love, to a company of horses
in Pharaoh's chariots."—CANTICLES, I., 9.
‡ "Turn away thine eyes from me, for they have overcome
me."—CANTICLES, VI., 5.

68.
As though her touch were exquisite,
Instinct with magic power ;
A superhuman attribute,
That tingled him all o'er.

69.
"And I love you!" she softly said,
Kissing his crimson cheek.
Marvelling why it should be red
While she grew pale and weak.

70.
Emotions both elate and tire
And play upon the soul,
As they who play upon the lyre
Its melodies control.

71.
And what is FEELING but a song ?
And what is LOVE but praise ?
Angelic harmony—so long
As our good angel plays.

72.
When *Jacob* first his *Rachel* spied
(Like a new element)
He lifted up his voice and cried
With joy and ravishment.

73.
The fulness of his heart o'erflow'd
In tears of tenderness ;
Unutterable love he vow'd,
And plighted with a kiss.

74.
The man born blind who saw the sun
(And bless'd the vision bright
He could not cease to look upon)
Knew not such sweet delight.

75.
So fondly—freely—faithfully—
Was each the other's pride,*
And so it came to pass to be
With Bardolph and his bride.†

---

* "My beloved is fair and ruddy—the *chiefest among ten thousand.*"—CANTICLES, V., 10.
† "My dove, my undefiled, is *unique ;* she is *the choice one* of her mother's children."—CANTICLES, VI., 9.

76.

In mutual adoration, they,
    Enchanted, spend the hour ;
Mid smiles, and tears, and feigned play,
    Their gushing souls they pour.

77.

Each trifle toyed with romance,
    The height and depth were levell'd ;
All nature mov'd as if to dance—
    The whole creation revell'd.

78.

For when love joins congenial hearts,
    Connubial bliss is heaven ;
And Heaven's Lord His aid imparts
    To cheer the gladness given.

79.

Not only clears its azure sky
    From the dark realm of night,
But tints, and makes it beautify
    Even the glorious light.

80.

The very air a balm assumes,
    Breathing a sense of peace ;
And adding fragrance to perfumes
    Which otherwise we miss.

81.

O joy of joys !   O vital spark
    Even in veins of flint !
O light that dwellest in the dark
    That knows not what is in't !*

82.

Electric fluid—all unseen—
    Unfelt until awoke !
O sainted cause, why even sin
    May be slain by thy shock !†

83.

Mysterious fire— yet unborn
    Until thy parents meet·
The Good and Beautiful—Self torn
    In order thee to greet !

---

* "The light shineth in darkness ; and the darkness comprehended it not."—"The true light, which lighteth every man that cometh into the world."—John I., 5, 9.

† " He that loveth not, knoweth not God, for God is love." "And every one that loveth, is born of God, and knoweth God."—1 John IV., 7, 8.

84.
Parent and babe at once thou art
Of all our happiness—
Awake—appear—keep not apart—
Beam forth—emblazon—bless!
    *   *   *   *

85.
And *they* were blest—*their* love was heaven—
However short the time,
In that short time to them was given
That which makes life sublime.

86.
Heart burns—ill humours—sordid hoard
Invaded not their hearth ;
At bed and board did they accord,
All their young life was mirth.

87.
Mirth innocent—mirth always kind—
Mirth springing like a well,
From depths which show'd the sky behind—
Love—inexhaustible !
    *   *   *   *

88.
In course of time, a seraph son
Was given, and then taken ;
Then came two daughters one by one
To cheer them thus forsaken.

89.
But Bardolph, who so mourn'd his sire,
So sorrow'd for that son,
That it reviv'd the smoulder'd fire
That gnaw'd his life upon.

90.
Except that being older grown,
Accustom'd to reflect,
He would not go and grieve alone,
Nor those he lov'd deject.

91.
He learn'd his trials to endure,
Not only as a man,
But as a godlike warrior,
Proud to bear all he can.

92.
Shoulder to shoulder, as it were,
With some one out of sight :
A pattern hero seen somewhere
Who taught him how to fight.

93.

He could not, would not spurn his grief,
    Nor labor to forget ;
He only sought to find relief
    In an example set.

94.

He could not, would not close that gulph,
    That earthquake in his soul ;
That dark abyss that drown'd his bliss,
    Defying self control.

95.

He could not, would not strive to blind
    His eyes to that torn page ;
The just affections of his mind
    To slay—were sacrilege.

96.

All that he could, all that he did
    Was, to that unseen sight
For explanation and for aid
    Appeal with all his might.

97.

The pangs which brought him near to God,
    The " treasures " hid in Him,
Bridg'd o'er the length of life's rough road
    With hopes beyond life's time.

98.

Not that they wean'd his fondness from
    The angels of his home ;
He thought *for them* in days to come
    With him beyond the tomb.

99.

For children—wife—(his wealth of life)
    Mother and brother too ;
His care, not less for all his grief,
    But all the greater grew.

100.

In public duties, he took care
    To be at least exact ;
He studied still the art of war,
    And how good leaders act.

101.

His people—knights—and soldiery
    Were happy in his rule ;
Happy and proud, ever to be
    Train'd in his loyal school.

102.

Repeatedly to foreign parts
    He took a chosen train,
To study all the useful arts
    And martial skill to gain.

103.

Lord Bardolph was about two years
    The junior of the king,*
Who, of the *late lord*, it appears,
    Hurried the burying.†

104.

And as in *Scotland he* last serv'd
    With that unhappy prince,
So for the *son* it was reserv'd
    His prowess to evince

105.

In *Ireland*, when he, with the king,
    The rebel Irish quell'd,‡
While that dread storm was gathering
    With which he was assail'd.

106.

In *England*, soon as they return'd
    To an unlook'd for fate,
Where *Lancaster* and *Percy* earn'd
    Every true patriot's hate.

107.

And dearly *Percy* duly paid
    The forfeit of his crime,
Involving, as he surely did,
    His friends in after time.

108.

But we forestall, and must recall
    The reader to the fact
Of the *Lord William Bardolph's* call
    In Scottish war to act

109.

The year before he died.— His widow,
    Then in her prime of life,
To the *Sir Thomas Mortimer*
    Became again a wife.

---

* King Richard II.
† William Lord Bardolph died soon after the Scottish campaign.
‡ King Richard was in Ireland, both to quell rebellion and avenge the death of his viceroy, relative and heir apparent and presumptive, Roger Mortimer, the Earl of March, killed by the rebels.

110.

This was that Lady Agnes who
Selected Avice Cromwell
For her son Lord Bardolph—she who
Was daughter to Lord Michael

111.

Poynings, related to the *Mowbrays*
And to *Sir Thomas Poynings*
(Who *Lord St John* was in after days)
One of the three husbandings

112.

Of *Mortimer Philippa*, sister
To the wife of *Hotspur*
And to the *Lord Roger Mortimer*,
King Richard's rightful heir.

113.

And these relationships so near'd
Lord Bardolph to them all,
That to their fortunes he appear'd
For good, or ill, in thrall.

114.

By his own father's mother, he
(Bardolph) had royal blood ;
Both to the king and Mortimer
In that relation stood.

115.

Besides which, all his ancestry
Were loyal to the line
Of legal heirs, and us'd to see
The royal favor shine.

116.

The King—Lord Bardolph—Mortimer—
From the First Edward came ;
Earl Percy and his son Hotspur
Claim'd parentage the same.

117.

Only the king came son by son,
The others by a mother ;
And these were interlink't as one
By marriage with each other.

118.

Hotspur's wife was Elizabeth,
The heir apparent's sister ;
And well might he set life and death
Against the vile Lancaster—

119.

Of whom anon.—We know full well
That bad men prosper in
This world, to be made ripe for hell,
By adding sin to sin.

120.

Therefore, the outrages which happen
Need not surprise too much ;
God will, in time, draw His sword sharp on
Them who His servants touch.

NOTES TO PART II.

VERSE 22.

Sir Ralph Cromwell, lord of the Castle and Manor of Tatsall, or Tattersale, Lincolnshire.

=In the 47th of Edward III. he was retained to serve the king in his wars beyond the seas, with twenty men at arms, and twenty archers, of which two to be knights, besides himself, and nine esquires.

= In the 10th of Richard II. he was a Banneret, and retained to serve the king in defence of the realm against an invasion then feared; as also in the 8th of Richard II. to serve him in the wars of Scotland.

=Having been summoned to Parliament from 49th Edward III. until 22nd Richard II., he departed this life 27th August, the same year (1399); leaving Maud his wife surviving, and Ralph his son and heir, thirty years of age; and three daughters—

Avicia Lady Bardolph,
Maud Lady Fitzwilliam,
Elizabeth Lady Clifton,
and afterwards Bensted.

VERSE 88.

=Thomas Lord Bardolph was born at Birling, in Sussex (one of the manors of his father, and eventually his own, and part of the dower of his mother, Lady Agnes Poynings-Bardolph,) on or about the 22nd December, 1368.

=He made proof of his age in the 13th year of Richard II. (1390).

=After his marriage, and during his yet minority, he resided with his father-in-law, Ralph Lord Cromwell, at Lord Cromwell's Castle of Tatsall, or Tattershall, in Lincolnshire, in the hundred of Gartree; and there his children were born, as appears from the records of their births and baptisms.

=It was, it seems, the custom of the great barons of England, in those days, to purchase the wardship or guardianship of some young orphan heir or heiress for the purpose of marrying the same to the guardian's own son or daughter. In this way, the Lord *Michael Poynings* purchased the wardship of the last *William* Lord Bardolph, of Philippa Queen of England, in the year 1366 (40th Edward III.), for the sum of one thousand marks, in order that he might marry his own daughter *Agnes*, who thus became Lady Bardolph, and afterwards Lady Mortimer. And, in like manner, it appears that *Ralph* Lord Cromwell had secured the betrothal of *Thomas* Lord Bardolph to his daughter *Avicia*, so that they were married while yet under age, and indeed so early that at the birth of *Joan*, their youngest daughter, 12th November, 1390 (14th Richard II.), the youthful father himself had not yet completed two and twenty years.

VERSE 103.

=William Lord Bardolph, son of John Lord Bardolph and Elizabeth (daughter of Elizabeth de Clare, the granddaughter of King Edward I.), was left an orphan at the age of fourteen years (5th August, 1363), 37th Edward III., in the wardship of Sir Michael, otherwise Lord Michael, Poynings.

=On the 13th of June, in the 8th of King Richard II., he was summoned by writ to meet the King with his horses, and arms, and whole service, on the 14th of July, to march into Scotland against the Scots; and he died in the following year, 29th January, 1386 (9th Richard II.), leaving his son *Thomas* his next heir, and sixteen years old on Friday next after the feast of St. Thomas last past.

=The will of William Bardolph, Lord of Wyrmygey, bears date at his manor of Caythorpe, in Lincolnshire, 12th September, 1385 (9th Richard II.), by which he bequeathed his body to be buried in the quire of the church of the Friars of the Order of Mount Carmel, at Lynn, which was situate on the banks of the river *Lynn* (or Nar), between the South Gate and Alhallows Church, and is said to have been a foundation of the (William) Lord Bardolph in 1269, conjointly with the Lord Scales of Middleton, and Sir John Wiggenhall.

=The only legacy recorded is one to his heir male (Thomas) of a part of the very cross of Our Lord, set in gold, and which probably had been presented to his father (John) by Pope Clement.

=William Lord Bardolph was summoned to Parliament from the 20th January, 1376 (49th Edward III.), to the 3rd September, 1385 (9th Richard II.).

The following seal impressions are tangible relics of the *Bardolph* family, too interesting to be omitted, as well as apposite and opportune to the foregoing memoranda of these two last Lords Bardolph of Wyrmygey.

The annexed engraving is from an impression of a seal of *Thomas* lord Bardolph attached to a deed dated 4 August (14th Richard II.), (now in the possession of the Rev. C. R. Manning, Rector of Diss, Norf.), and purporting to be a grant and license from Thomas Bardolph, Lord of Wyrmygeye, to the master and chaplains of Norton Soupecorse, or Subcourse, of the castle of Mettingham, near Bungay, Suffolk, with divers lands at Mettingham and Ilketishale (or Bardolph's Hall).

There is also another grant and license from *William* Lord Bardolph to the college of Mettingham of Mettingham castle, dated 5th February (6th Richard II.).

== The four ensuing seal impressions of the *Bardolph* family are attached to deeds in the possession of Sir Thomas Hare, Baronet, of Stow Bardolph Hall, who has kindly permitted their use : and for the information respecting each of them, the author is indebted to the Rev. George Dashwood, Rector of Stow Bardolph, near Downham Market, Norfolk.

The first of these seals is that of *William* Bardolph, Lord of Wyrmygey, father of the last Lord *Thomas*, and it is attached to a deed which assigns a strip of land (at Downham) to one John Bokyngham, his superannuated trumpeter, (or "clariner,") and bears the date of 1380, being "given at Wyrmygey, on Monday, the feast of St. Barnabas the Apostle, in the third year of King Richard the Second."

The second of these seals is that of *John* Bardolph, Lord of Wyrmygey, father of *William*, and grandfather of *Thomas*, and it is attached to a deed bearing date (1347) 20th Edward III.

The third impression is that
of another seal of the same
John Lord Bardolph, attached
to a deed bearing date (1339)
12th Edward III.

And the fourth (anterior
to them all) is that of *John*
Bardolph of *Frettenham*, a
member of a branch of the
Bardolph family, and it is
attached to a deed bearing
date (1337) 10th Edward
III. But it is remarkable
for being charged with *five*
instead of three cinqfoils
on the shield.—(See the
Legend, part X., verses
51—54.)

This (sixth) seal impression is a copy of one attached to a deed in the possession of the Rev. Jermyn Pratt, of Ryston Hall, near Downham, Norfolk; and appears to represent a Bardolph knight and charger in career; or, at least, caparisoned for action.

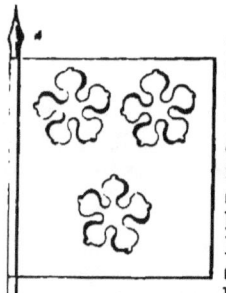

Finally. The annexed engraving represents the Bardolph banner, or battle flag, as described in an ancient poem, which, after the style of Homer, enumerates the leaders of the forces who were present at the siege of Carlaverock, in Scotland, A.D. 1334 (32nd Edward I.). On that occasion, this standard distinguished the followers of *Hugh* Lord Bardolph, whose squadron formed part of the brigade of Henry de Lacey, Earl of Lincoln. The same Lord Hugh (son of William Lord Bardolph and Juliana de Gournai his wife) was then about forty-nine years of age, and one hundred years anterior to the time of his descendant, the last Lord Thomas. The poem thus makes mention of Lord Hugh:

" Hue Bardoulf, de grant maniere
 Riches hommes, preus, e courtois
En azure quint fuelles trois
 Portoit de fin or esmere."

(AUTHOR'S TRANSLATION.)

" Bardolph! with his noble bearing—
With his knights, rich, bland, and bold—
All, his badge so fond of wearing—
Azure field, three cinqfoils gold."

As for the meaning of the antique word *esmere*, it seems to contrast with *molu*, or *moulu*, thus—

or moulu=dead, or ground gold ;
or esmere=bright, or burnished gold.

VERSES 116—118.

In the year 1381, there departed this life, at Cork, *Edmund Mortimer*, 3rd Earl of March, the King's Lieutenant, or Viceroy, in Ireland. He was also Marshall of England, and, in right of his wife, Earl of Ulster, and Gloster, and Lord of Clare and Connaught. He was a man of amiable and elevated character ; and, being born in 1351, was only thirty years of age.

His wife, Philippa Plantagenet, was the only daughter and heiress of Lyonnell Duke of Clarence, third son of King Edward the Third, and next heir, after King Richard II., to the crown.

Their children were as follows :

1. Roger Mortimer, 4th Earl of March, heir apparent and presumptive of England, who married Eleanor, daughter of Thomas Holland, Earl of Kent, half-brother to King Richard II.

2. Edmund Mortimer, who, in 1403, became both prisoner and son-in-law to Owen Glendower, Prince of Wales.

3. John de Mortimer, executed in the 3rd Henry VI.

4. Elizabeth Mortimer, wife to the celebrated, but ill-fated, Sir Henry Percy, otherwise Lord Henry Percy, and "Hotspur" ; and

5. Philippa Mortimer, whose third husband was John Poynings, Lord St. John, cousin to the Lady Agnes Poynings-Bardolph-Mortimer.

=In the year 1398, Roger Mortimer, 4th Earl of March, also became the King's Lieutenant, or Viceroy, in Ireland, and was slain in an encounter with the rebels, on St. Margaret's day, at Kenlys, in Leinster.

=In consequence of which, in the year 1399, being the 22nd or 23rd year of King Richard II., the same glorious King himself arrived at Waterford with 200

7

sail, upon a Sunday, and the morrow after St. Petro-
nil, or Pernil; and on the sixth day, in the same
week, at Ford, in Kenlys, within the county of Kil-
dare, were slain of the Irish 200, by Jenicho and
other English; and the morrow after, the Dublinians
made a rode in the county of O'Bryn, and slew of
the Irish 33, and took prisoners 80 men, women and
children.

=In the same year, the King came to Dublin, the
fourth day before the Calends of July, where he
heard rumours of Henry Duke of Lancaster his coming into England, whereupon he passed over with
speed into England.

The following genealogical table may afford some idea (though imperfect) of the relationship of the *Bardolph* family with the other royal kindreds of *de Burgh*, *de Clare*, *Plantagenet*, *Mortimer*, *Poynings*, and *Percy*; and of the links between King Edward the First and King Edward the Fourth, with reference to the terrific Wars of the Two Roses—YORK and LANCASTER :—

Edward (Plantagenet) the First, King of England.=Eleanor, Queen of England, daughter of Ferdinand III. and sister of Alphonso King of Castile.

Gilbert de Clare, 7th Earl of Hertford, 3rd Earl of Gloster, commonly called, The Red de Clare.=Joan Plantagenet, second daughter, born at Acra, in Palestine, A.D. 1272.

Gilbert de Clare, married Maud, daughter of Richard de Burgh, Earl of Ulster; died 5th Edward II.

John de Burgh, son of Richard de Burgh, Earl of Ulster, 1st husband; died 1313.=Elizabeth de Clare, foundress of Clare Hall, Cambridge; died 34th Edward III.; buried in the Priory church at Ware.=Roger Lord D'Aumari, or d'Amorie,* 3rd husband; died 15th Edward II.; buried in the Priory church at Ware.

Maud Plantagenet, daughter of Henry Plantagenet, Earl of Lancaster, aunt to first Earl Percy.=William de Burgh and de Clare Earl of Ulster, &c.; born 1312; murdered 1333.

Elizabeth de Clare and de Burgh, daughter and co-heir; died 4th November, 1360.=John Lord Bardolph, "De Wyrmygey"; died 3rd Aug., 1363.

Lyonell Duke of Clarence, Earl of Ulster, Gloster, Clare, in right of his wife, 3rd son of Edward III.; died 1368; buried at Clare.=Elizabeth de Burgh and de Clare; born 1332; married 1352; died 1362; buried in the church of the Augustine Friars, Clare, in Suffolk.

Agnes de Fovnings, Bardolph and Mortimer, cousin of Thomas Poynings, Lord St. John, daughter of Michael Lord Poynings.=William Lord Bardolph, "De Wyrmygey"; buried at King's Lynn, 1386.

Edmund Mortimer, 3rd Earl of March, Marshall of England, Lieutenant of Ireland, Earl of Ulster, Lord of Clare, and Connaught in right of his wife; born 1351; died 1381.=Philippa Plantagenet, only daughter; born 1355; heiress of England, de Clare, de Burgh, Ulster, Connaught, &c.

Avicia, daughter of Ralph Lord Cromwell; died 1st July, 1421.=Thomas Lord Bardolph, "De Wyrmygey"; killed at Bramham Moor, Sunday, February 19th, 1408.

Anne Lady Clifford and Cobham; left no children. Her husband's nephew, Thomas Lord Clifford, married Elizabeth Percy, the only daughter of "Hotspur."=Joan Lady Phelip and "Bardolph"; left one daughter Elizabeth "Beaumont."

a

a

Roger Mortimer, 4th Earl of March, heir of England; born 3rd April, 1374; married Eleanor, daughter of the Earl of Kent, half-brother to King Richard II.

Edmund Mortimer, prisoner and son-in-law of Owen Glendor, Prince of Wales, 1103, with his nephew and namesake.

Elizabeth Mortimer, the wife of "Hotspur," whose father's mother, Lady Mary Plantagenet, was grand-daughter of Edmund Crouchback, and great-grand-daughter to King Henry III.

Philippa Mortimer; married 1, Earl of Pembroke; 2, Earl of Arundel; 3, Thomas Poynings, Lord St. John, cousin of Agnes Lady Bartolph and Mortimer.

Edmund Mortimer, 5th Earl of March, heir of England; born 8th November, 1392; died 13th January, 1416, without issue. He was at the battle of *Agincourt*, on Friday, 25th October, 1415, where he commanded a retinue of 60 men at arms, 19 lances, and 160 archers; of whom were 1 banneret, 3 knights, and 55 esquires.

Roger; born 9th April, 1394; no issue.

Anne; born 21st December, 1389; heiress of England; married Richard Plantagenet, Earl of Cambridge, Duke of York, son of Edmund of Langley, 5th son of Edward III.

Eleanor.

Their son Richard, Earl of March, and Cambridge, and Duke of York, heir of England, was the father of

Edward (Plantagenet) the Fourth, King of England.

* d'Amorie—Lord of Sandall, Yorks. and Haighton, Oxon. and Fawkeshal, Surrey. &c.

Constable of Knaresborough Castle. Governor of Glocester Castle and Corfe Castle. Warden of the Forest of Purbeck.

WERMIGEY.

PART III.

KING RICHARD II. *versus* KING HENRY IV.,

OR

FRIENDSHIPS TRUE AND FALSE.

" *Duke of York.*—Long live King Henry, of that name
    the Fourth !
" *Bishop of Carlisle.*—Oh ! forbid it God !
That in a christian climate, souls refin'd
Should show so heinous, black, obscene a deed !
I speak to subjects, and a subject speaks,
Stirr'd up by Heaven thus boldly for his King.
My lord of Hereford here, whom you call King,
Is a foul traitor to proud Hereford's King,
And, if you crown *him*, let me prophesy—
The blood of English shall manure the ground,
And future ages groan for this foul act.
Peace shall go sleep with Turks and Infidels,
And, in this seat of Peace, tumultuous wars
Shall kin with kin, and kind with kind confound ;
Disorder, horror, fear, and mutiny
Shall here inhabit, and this land be call'd
The Field of Golgotha and dead men's skulls.
Oh ! if you rear this House against this House
It will the wofullest division prove
That ever fell upon this cursed earth.
Prevent—resist it—let it not be so,
Lest child, child's children, cry against you—Woe ! "
            SHAKESPEARE. *Richard II.*, Act IV., Sc. 1.

1.

King Edward died—his valiant son
    Already was no more ;
The Black Prince left his father's throne
    To his inheritor.

2.

Richard the Second reign'd instead,
  Their representative ;
Yet could not these illustrious dead
  Insure him long to live.

3.

The sire cannot invest the son
  With jealous Nature's power,
Nor can the sire prevent his son
  Accepting Nature's dower.

4.

Each has his gift particular,
  King Richard needed *one*,
To wit—that strength of character
  Which in his father shone.

5.

Not without courage *now* and *then*,
  Not without tact or skill ;
Not wanting in goodwill to men,
  But in a wise goodwill.

6.

Too fond of ease and soft delights,
  Too full of simple trust ;
His chief companions " carpet knights,"
  While his good sword got rust.

7.

So many a fairly nurtur'd lad,
  Himself both good and kind,
The fool's or villain's dupe is made,
  And then to shame consign'd.

8.

Not, indeed, of necessity,
  Since all may ask of God,
Who, of His liberality,
  Giveth each needful good.

9.

And would we ask, we might receive
  The *extras* we most want ;
But creatures scorning to believe,
  Can their Creator grant ?

10.

For, as in wedlock, two must wed,
  And *each* must give consent,
So, if a boon be borrowed,
  One lends—one wants it lent.

11.

Not that to every foolish whim
　The wise Eternal bends,
But that He will be found of him
　Who seeks the Best of Friends.

12.

'Tis gross neglect endangers all!
　Creatures we serve and love,
But Him we like not to recall
　In whom we live and move.

13.

Obliquity—perversity
　We choose, by that " Freewill "
Of which we boast, only to be
　Our own destroyers still!

14.

O for that Bubbling Fount within
　Of which the Saviour speaks,
That he will cause to quench all sin
　In him who for it seeks.

15.

O for that " Sword," and for that " Shield,"
　And for that " Great Reward "
Religion promises to yield
　To those who love their " Lord! "

16.

To evil men, to human fiends
　The weak must fall a prey,
Unless God's power frustrate their ends,
　And we ask " day by day."

17.

King Richard—(ah! who'd be a king
　Without God's panoply!)—
King Richard fell, and felt the sting
　Of foul men's flattery.

18.

His cousin, Henry Bolingbroke
　(The traitor of this tale)
First Earl of Derby, and then Duke
　Of Hereford as well—

19.

Son of the Duke of Lancaster,
　Call'd John of Gaunt, or Ghent—
Daring to wish the crown to wear.
　On seizing it was bent

8

20.
First he accus'd another Duke
Of similar design,
And, by the duel, undertook
To prove his charge malign.

21.
Thomas de Mowbray was the man,
The Duke of Norfolk then,
On whom he grounded his vile plan,
Hoping to have him slain.

22.
Norfolk in vain the charge denied,
Protesting as he might,
But still he offer'd to abide
The issue of a fight.

23.
King Richard doubted, disbeliev'd,
Yet fearing such intent
In either one might be achiev'd,
Sent both to banishment.

24.
De Mowbray died of broken heart,
But not so Hereford,
Cause he alleg'd why he should start
A rebel from abroad.

25.
Soon as his father was deceas'd,
He took his father's name ;
As banish'd *Hereford* he ceas'd,
As *Lancaster* he came.

26.
The king was *weak*, the next heir *dead*,
Leaving his son a *child* ;
Why should not Lancaster succeed?
Why not the king be kill'd ?

27.
If great Earl Percy could be caught
By a well-varnish'd *ruse*,
" That he was wrong'd, and *only sought*
His right," him he could use

28.
To mount the summit and the height
Which his ambition dar'd,
Then kick the ladder down, and fight
The fool thus made and scar'd !

29.

Such prov'd the case; and when too late
  The traitorous deed was done—
The *weak* king kill'd, and the *bad* sate
  Defiant on his throne.

30.

Percy deplor'd the part he play'd,
  Which he could not recal—
Richard, by murder, was now dead,
  And the young heir in thrall!

31.

Unworthy friends too often prove
  The bitterest of foes;
So Hereford's and Percy's love
  Begat their direst woes.

32.

Both join'd to thrust King Richard down
  And speed him to his fate;
And after he was dead and gone,
  Their love turn'd into hate.

33.

There was *a Bishop* in those days –
  (Glory surround his name!)
There was *one Bishop* earn'd a praise
  Which put the rest to shame.

34.

There was *a* Bishop—*only one,*
  (I pray you mark it well!)
Who, when King Richard lost his throne,
  Would not his own soul sell!

35.

Stood by *him* in the hour of need
  As only good men dare;
Forbade the traitor to succeed,
  And spurn'd him without fear.

36.

Defied the penalty incurr'd,
  Recking nought but the right;
Siding with him who wrong endur'd
  With all his honest might.

37.

No solemn mockery of " Law,"
  No sophistry, no guile,
Could cheat, or coax, or overawe
  THE BISHOP OF CARLISLE.

38.

God bless the man, in heaven high!
Although the modern creed
Might make " an action on me lie,"
For " praying for the dead! "

39.

God bless the man, in heaven high!
Let men on earth revere
Him who then stood the good cause by
While thieves and rogues " cashier."

40.

While murder mask'd its vile intent
To slay the sovereign ;
While treason tried to circumvent
With treason's reasoning—

41.

He, in his place in Parliament
(Having the right to speak),
Made protest plain and vehement
To the strong *for* the weak.

42.

What though that speech availed him not,
But rather speeded fate,
It never never was forgot,
And bore its fruit, though late.

43.

To men like Bardolph it was dear,
It cheer'd him in his " vote "
To " save " the king from what was clear
They meant should be his lot.

44.

What though no Bishop on the Bench
Supported brother Mercks,*
It wrought in many a conscience
Conscience's pricks and irks.

45.

It stirr'd the generous to rebel,
It sooth'd each loyal breast ;
It never ceas'd the base to tell
They never should have rest.

46.

It clear'd the motives and the minds
Of those who were not clear,
To see through all the sorry blinds
Of interest and fear.

---

* Thomas Mercks, Bishop of Carlisle.

47.

Amid the falsehood of this world,
  God will have truth to shine;
His flag of war must be unfurl'd,
  If men will make them twine.

48.

From Bolingbroke, Earl Percy woke
  To find out what he was;
And that himself had been the hook
  On which hung his bad cause.

49.

Besides the *murder* of the king,
  And *ruling in his stead;*
Besides *the next heir jockeying,*
  (Whose aunt Hotspur had wed)—

50.

This heir, young Edmund Mortimer,
  Fighting the Walish prince,
By him was made a prisoner,
  And kept a prisoner since.

51.

In vain the Percys sued the king
  To rescue the young man,
Or aid them in recovering—
  He jeer'd at either plan.

52.

"The young heir, and his sisters two,
  Were better in the grave;
They made by far too much ado—
  The kingdom they would have."

53.

Such undisguis'd ingratitude,
  Such ruthless lust of power,
Sufficiently his temper show'd,
  But soon he showed it more.

54.

The Percys fought at Homeldon,
  And overcame the Scot;
Ten thousand laid upon the ground,
  Five hundred captives got.

55.

Douglas their gallant chieftain too,
  Which would a ransom bring,
Enough to ransom EDMUND, who
  Was England's rightful king.

56.

The ready *Lancaster* sent word
  They should *not* have the prize.
" Such glorious booty ! by the Lord !
  The money should be his ! "

57.

The wolf ! the barefac'd man of blood !
  What next appropriate ?
No man might eat his daily food,
  Or live on his estate !

58.

Incens'd beyond endurance, then
  The Percy's form'd a plan,
Rather to make the foe their friend
  Than yield to such a man.

59.

Rather the noble *Douglas* free
  Than make him Henry's slave ;
Rather help Wales to liberty
  Than such a tyrant have.

60.

The league was made, the terms agreed,
  Wales by Glendôr be rul'd ;
Edmund to England south succeed,
  Percy the north should hold.

61.

Young Edmund Mortimer, whose aunt
  Was the brave Hotspur's bride,
Full glad was of a lieutenant
  So zealous on his side.

62.

Nor " north," nor " south," could he e'er own,
  Nor save himself from thrall ;
Freedom and kingdom must be won
  By Hotspur, if at all.

63.

Hotspur's own uncle, Worcester's Earl,
  More ready than his father
The tyrant from his throne to hurl,
  His forces he would gather.

64.

Thus Hotspur—Worcester—Mortimer
  Uniting their array
With Bardolph, Douglas, and Glendôr,
  Would try to win the day.

65.

" Hotspur," Earl Percy's valiant son,
  The hero of the north,
As chief commander all would own,
  To lead the powers forth.

66.

King Henry, ever on the watch,
  Pursued a wary course ;
Fearing the Percys, Welsh, and Scotch,
  Northwest advanc'd a force.

VERSES 21—24.
THOMAS MOWBRAY, DUKE OF NORFOLK.

" In the year 1301, Roger Bigod, Earle of Norfolke, ordained King Edward (the First) to be his heire, and when he departed this life without issue, King Edward the Second honored his own half-brother, Thomas of Brotherton, (a younger son of King Edward the First by his second wife Margaret, sister of Philip the Faire, King of France,) with the titles of *Marshall* and *Earle* of Norfolke, whose daughter Margaret, called *Marshallesse* and *Countess* of Norfolke, was wife to John Lord Segrave; and King Richard the Second created her *Dutchess* of Norfolke; and the same day, he created *Thomas Mowbray*, her daughter's sonne, the Earl of Nottingham, the first Duke of Norfolke, and Earl Marshall of England. This is hee that, before the King, was challenged and accused by Henry of *Lancaster*, Duke of Hereford, for uttering inconsiderately certain reprochfull and derogatory words against the King; and when they were to fight a combat, at the very barre and entry of the lists, by the voice of a herald it was proclaimed in the King's name, *that both of them should be banished for ever;* who afterwards ended his life at Venice, leaving *two sonnes* behind him in England, of which Thomas Earle Marshall and of Nottingham, for no other title had he, was *beheaded* for seditious plotting against Henry of Lancaster, who had now possessed himself of the crowne by the name of King Henry the Fourth; but his brother and heir John was, in the reign of Henry the Sixth, reinstated in his father's honors, as his brother's heire."—*Camden's Britannia, Northfolke, p.* 182-3.

VERSE 27.
HENRY PERCY, EARL OF NORTHUMBERLAND.

" William de Percie came into England with William the Conqueror, and was descended from the Earls of Brabant. The first of this family that was made Earl of Northumberland was Henry Percie, the son of Mary, daughter of Henry Earl of Lancaster. This nobleman signalized his valour in the wars under Edward the Third, and was by him rewarded with large possessions in Scotland. He was very much enriched by his second wife Matilda Lucy, who obliged him to bear the arms of the Lucies; and by Richard the Second was created Earl of Northumberland. His behaviour was very ungrateful to this his great benefactor, for he deserted him in his straits, and helped Henry the Fourth to the crown. He had the Isle of Man bestowed on him by this king, against whom he also rebelled, being pricked in conscience at the unjust deposing of King Richard, and vexed at the close confinement of (the undoubted heir of the crown) Edmund Mortimer, Earl of March, his kinsman. Hereupon he first sent some forces against him under the command of his brother, Thomas Earl of Worcester, and his own forward son Henry, surnamed Hot-spur, who were both slain in the battel at Shrewsbury. Upon this he was attainted of high treason ; but presently received again into the seeming favour of the king, who indeed stood in awe of him. He had also his estate and goods restored to him, except only the Isle of Man, which the king took back into his own hand. Yet not long after, the popular and heady man again proclaimed war against the king as an usurper, having called in the Scots to his assistance. And now, leading on the rebels in person, he was surprized by Thomas Rokesby, High Sheriff of Yorkshire, at Barham-moor, where in a confused skirmish his army was routed, and himself slain, in the year 1408.—*Camden's Britannia, Northumberland, p. 867.*

VERSES 33—47.
BISHOP MERCKS.

" It was about this time (A.D. 1399—1400) moved in Parliament what should be done with King Richard? (for he was not yet murthered :) whereupon *Thomas Mercks*, Bishop of *Carlisle*, a learned man and wise, and who had never given allowance to the deposing of King Richard, now that he was in a place of freedom of speech, rose up and said :—

" My lords : the matter now to be propounded is of marvellous weight and consequence ; wherein there are two points chiefly to be considered : the *First*, whether King *Richard* be sufficiently put out of his throne ? the *Second*, whether the duke of *Lancaster* be lawfully taken in ? For the first ; How can that be sufficiently done, where there is no power sufficient to do it ? The Parliament cannot, for of the Parliament, the king is the head ; and can the body put down the head ? You will say, But the head may bow itself down, and the king may resign. It is true : but what force is in that (resignation) which is made by force? and who does not know that King Richard's resignation was no other? But suppose, he be sufficiently put out? yet how comes the duke of *Lancaster* to be lawfully in? If you say by conquest, you speak treason; for what conquest without arms? and can a subject take arms against his lawful sovereign? and not be treason? If you say, by election of the state, you speak not reason: for what power hath the state to elect, while any is living that hath right to succeed? But such a successor is *not* the duke of *Lancaster*, as descended from *Edmund Crouchback*, the *elder* son of King *Henry* the Third, though put by from the crown for deformity of his body: for who knows not the falseness of this allegation? seeing it is a thing notorious, that this *Edmund* was neither the *elder* brother, nor *crookbackt* (though called so for some other reason), but a goodly personage, and without any deformity.* And yourselves cannot forget a thing so lately done, as *who it was that*, in the fourth year of King Richard, *was declared by Parliament to be the heir to the crown*, in case King Richard should die without issue. But why, then, is not this claim made? Because *Silent Leges inter Arma*. What disputing of titles can there be against the stream of power? But, howsoever, it is extreme injustice, that King *Richard* should be condemned without being heard, or once allowed to make his defence.—And now, my lords, I have spoken thus at this time, that you may consider before it be too late: For as yet it is in your power to undo that justly, which you have unjustly done.

" Such was the Bishop's speech, but to as little purpose as if he had gone about to bring back yesterday. He was himself arrested by the Marshal, and committed to prison in the Abbey of *St. Albans;* but afterwards, without further censure, set at liberty,— till, upon a conspiracy of Lords, wherein he was a party, he was condemned to die, though through

---

* The word *crouch-back* appears to be susceptible of a double meaning; or else to have been substituted for the word *cross'd-back;* this Edmund, like the king his brother, being a *crusader*, and, perhaps, more than others noted for wearing the sacred symbol on his back, as the crusaders did, and as the Roman Catholic hierarchs still do, on some occasions. The author remembers to have seen (A.D. 1820) at Notre Dame, in Paris, some splendid robes, thus figured, stiff with gold embroidery, and presented by the First Napoleon. There was also once an order of monks called " crouched," or " crutchet friars," a term still designating a well-known locality in London.

extremity of grief, he prevented execution."—See
Sir Richard Baker's Chronicle of the Kings of England. Reign of Henry IV.

VERSE 50.
OWEN GLENDOR.

" Of the famous Owen Glyn-dwr, or Glyn-Dowrdwy,
I find the following account in some notes of the
learned and judicious antiquary, Robert Vaughan, of
Hengwrt, Esq.: "Sir Davidh Gam was wholly devoted to the interest of the Duke of Lancaster; upon
which account it was, that Owen ap Gruffyth Vychan
(commonly call'd Owen Glyn-dwr) was his mortal
enemy. This Owen had his education at one of the
Inns of Court, and was preferr'd to the service of
King Richard II., whose *scutifer* (as Walsingham
saith) he was. Owen, being assured that his king
and master Richard was deposed and murder'd, and
withall provoked by several affronts and wrongs done
him by the Lord Grey of Ruthin his neighbour,
whom King Henry very much countenanced against
him, took arms, and looking upon Henry as an
usurper, caus'd himself to be proclaim'd Prince of
Wales. And though himself were descended pater-
nally but from a younger brother of the house of
Powis, yet (as ambition is ingenious) he finds out a
way to lay claim to the principality, as descended
(by a daughter) from Lhewelyn ap Gruffydh, the
last Prince of the British race. He invaded the
lands, burnt and destroyed the houses and estates of
all those that favour'd and adher'd to King Henry.
He call'd a Parliament to meet at Machynlheth, in
Montgomeryshire; whither the nobility and gentry
of Wales came, in obedience to his summons; and
among them the said *David Gam*, but with an intention to murder *Owen*. The plot being discover'd,
and he taken before he could put it into execution,
he was like to have suffer'd as a traitor: but inter-
cession was made for him by Owen's best friends and
the greatest upholders of Owen's cause; whom he
could not either honourably or safely deny. Yet
notwithstanding this pardon, as soon as he return'd
to his own country, where he was a man of consider-
able interest, he exceedingly annoy'd *Owen's* friends.
Not long after, Owen enter'd the Marches of Wales,
destroying all with fire and sword; and having then
burnt the house of *Sir David Gam*, 'tis reported he
spake thus to one of his tenants:

O gweli di wr coch cam,
Yn ynofyn y Gyrnigwen ;
Dywed y bôd hi tan y lan,
A nod y glo ar ei phen."
(author's version.)
Should you see blood-red Sir Gam
Seeking his white-horn'd ewe-lamb,
Tell him it is stretch'd and dead,
With a coal black branded head !
—See *Camden's Britannia, additions to Brecknockshire*,
p. 591.

A Welsh clergyman has kindly afforded the following explanation of the Welsh lines.

" The stanza of Owen Glyndwr is rather difficult
to understand, till we consider the time and circumstances of the person of whom it was uttered.

" David Gam was a prisoner of Glyndwr's, and all
his estate and palace near Brecon set on fire.

" Glyndwr meeting one of Sir David's friends, is
said to have composed the verse *impromptu*. This is
its translation :

" *If you see a red stooping man*
Looking for the whitehorned ewe,
Say she (it) is under the bank
With a brand of coal upon her (its) head."

" Most of the wealth of that age, you know, consisted of sheep and cattle. Therefore, I presume, the
verse was a sort of banter—that the lately stately
white palace, and fair estate of Sir David Gam, was
now in ruin, and a heap of ashes.—H. L. D."

The ensuing genealogical table shows the relationship and common descent, from King Henry III., of
some of the chief actors in the commencement of the
bloody tragedy of England's civil wars, namely :—

(1). King Richard II., of Bordeaux.

(2). Edmund Mortimer, 5th Earl of March, his
next of kin, and rightful heir.

(3). Thomas Mowbray, Duke of Norfolk.

(4.) King Henry IV., of Bolingbroke, Duke of
Lancaster, and Hereford, Earl of Derby, &c., *the*
usurper ; and

(5.) Henry Percy, first Earl of Northumberland,
the warning victim of *un*-duty (as regards Richard),
im-policy (as regards Hereford), and *in*-opportunity
(as regards the valiant but ill-fated " Hotspur.")

Henry III. (Plantagenet) King of England, reigned 36 years; died 16th November, 1272, aged 65.

Eleanor, the second of the five daughters of Raymond Count of Provence, married A.D. 1235. She survived him 19 years, and died a nun at Amoresbury.

Margaret of France, aged 18, and the king above 60 (being cousins), had two sons.

Edward I., called *Longshank*, died 7 July, 1307, aged 68, having reigned 34½ years.

Eleanor of Spain, his wife during 36 years, died A.D. 1291.

Edmund, called Earl of Lancaster, king of Sicily and Apulia, at Whitsuntide (24th Edward I) died A.D. 1296.

Crouchback, titular Blanche, daughter of Robert Count of Artois, brother of St. Louis King of France, widow of Henry of Champagne, King of Navarre.

Thomas, beheaded for treason.

John, and a sister, who both died in France.

Thomas of Brotherton, Earl of Norfolk and Marshal of England.

Margaret, wife of John lord Segrave, Marshaless and Duchess of Norfolk.

Edmund of Woodstock, Earl of Kent, was (by Margaret, the daughter of John, and sister of Thomas, Lord de Wake,) the father of

Edward II., dethroned and murdered (by his wife) 1327, aged 43.

Isabel of France, died at Castle Rising, Norfolk. A.D. 1357, aged 63.

Henry Earl of Derby, Duke of Lancaster.

Henry Earl of Derby, Duke of Lancaster.

1. Maud, wife of de Burgh, whose daughter married Lyonel.
2. Blanche, wife of Thomas Lord de Wake
3. Eleanor, wife of Richard Earl of Arundel.
4. Isabel, Prioress of Amoresbury.
5. Jane, wife of John Lord Moubray.
6. Mary, wife of Henry Lord Percy.

Elizabeth, wife of John, son of John Lord Moubray, and Jane of Lancaster.

Thomas de Moubray, Duke of Norfolk, died in exile.

Joan the Fair Maid of Kent, widow of Sir Thomas Holland, Earl of Kent.

Thomas Holland, Earl of Kent, Duke of Surrey.

Edward III., died of grief for his gallant son. 21 June, 1377, aged 64.

Philippa, of Hainault, married at York.

Blanche, the wife of John of Gaunt, to whom she brought these titles.

Edward the Blk. Prince, died A.D. 1376, aged 46.

Lyonel of Antwerp, Earl of Ulster, Duke of Clarence.

John of Gaunt, Earl of Richmond, Duke of Lancaster.

Edmund of Langley, Earl of Cambridge, Duke of York.

Thomas of Woodstock, Earl of Buckingham, Duke of Gloster, conspirator; died or put to death at Calais A.D. 1397.

the parents of Henry Percy, the first Earl of Northumberland, who, by Margaret Neville, was the father of the brave and celebrated "Hotspur."

Richard II., dethroned and murdered A.D. 1399.

Philippa Plantagenet, wife of Edmund Mortimer, 3rd Earl of March.

Henry IV., the conspirator and usurper.

Richard of Conyngsburg, who married Ann Mortimer.*

---

a   b   c

a   b   c

a. Thomas de Mowbray, Earl of Nottingham, beheaded A.D. 1405, by Henry IV.

b. Eleanor Holland, niece to King Richard II., his half-brother's daughter; died 23rd Dec., 1406, leaving her children heirs to the crown. = Roger Mortimer, Viceroy of Ireland, Heir of England, 4th Earl of March.

c. Philippa, wife of 1, Earl of Pembroke: 2, Earl of Arundel; 3, Thos. Poynings, 17 Lord St. John.

Edmund Mortimer, prisoner (with his namesake nephew) of Glendower, 17 June, 1402-3.

Elizabeth, = "Hotspur," whose son Henry, second Earl of Northumberland, had by Eleanor (daughter of Ralph Neville, Earl of Westmoreland, and Joan of Lancaster, his wife) nine sons.

Eleanor Mortimer, married Edward Courtenay, Earl of Devonshire, but left no issue.

Roger Mortimer born 9th April, 1394, at Netherwode, died without issue, buried in the Priory at Stoke.

Edmund Mortimer, 5th Earl of March, rightful heir of England, born 8th Nov., 1392, died 13th Jan., 1416. Present at the battle of Agincourt, 25th October, 1415. Married Anna, daughter of Edmund Earl of Stafford (killed at the battle of Shrewsbury), but left no issue.

Anne Mortimer, heiress of England, born 21st Dec., 1389. = Richard of Coningsburg (Plantagenet)* Earl of Cambridge, Duke of York, son of Edmund of Langley, godson of King Richard II.

Richard (Plantagenet) Earl of March and Cambridge, Duke of York, heir of England, born A.D. 1402, married Cecilia, daughter of Ralph Neville, Earl of Westmoreland.

Edward IV, Earl of March; his two sons murdered in the tower by their uncle Richard III.

Edmund, Earl of Rutland, barbarously stabbed after the battle at Wakefield, aged 12 years.

George Duke of Clarence, drowned in a butt of Malmsey wine by his two brothers.

Richard III., Duke of Gloster, killed at the battle of Bosworth, 20th Aug, 1485.

---

* Whose descendants supplanted the "usurper's" descendants, both by wedlock and by war,—each party unhappily accumulating crime until an unhallowed union produced that colossal development of wickedness, Henry VIII., after whom they both became extinct, according to the just judgment of God, the necessity of things, and the suicidal nature of sin. Study, and learn, all ye meaner creepers through all mean and crooked ways!

WERMIGEY.

PART IV.

CIVIL WAR—THE BATTLE OF SHREWSBURY.

21st July, 1403.

"So Israel rebelled against the House of David unto this day. And when all Israel heard that Jeroboam was come again, they made him king. And there was none that followed the House of David—but the tribe of Judah only."—1 Kings, xii., 19, 20.

1.

There were two roses—both were *pink*—
  Both grew upon one stem ;
The dew of heaven both did drink—
  Both bore one favor'd name.

2.

The one grew higher on the tree—
  It was, indeed, the crown ;
But slighted its own dignity,
  And bow'd too lowly down.

3.

The other wish'd to be the top—
  It had an envious face ;
And though its duty was to *prop*,
  It took the other's place.

4.

The humbled Rose wax'd *pale and wan*,
  Bleach'd by a sister's spite ;
The other grew to *crimson hue*,
  Burning with conscious guilt !

5.

It is a very common case,
  The same which first befel :
Cain envied Abel's happiness,
  And lost his own as well

10

6.

Adam and Eve were *not content*,
    They wish'd to be *as God*;
And so incurr'd the punishment
    Of banishment and blood.

7.

'Tis always so—men hate to know
    The everlasting truth—
That Wrong, or Right, they must forego,
    They cannot serve them both.

8.

That Wrong *may* triumph *for a time*,
    It is, indeed, allow'd—
To test, by fight, the Friends of Right,
    The faithful ones of God.

9.

He suffers all unrighteous wars,
    To make the wrong *confest*:
To prove those who will aid His cause,
    And clasp *them* to His breast.

10.

Just as a parent sees at play
    Children whose deeds he notes;
He lets the *wilful* have their way,
    But on the *dutrous* dotes.

11.

Bardolph had been confounded by
    Events which daunt the mind;
Had seen King Richard hounded by
    The basest of mankind.

12.

Richard! the son of such a sire
    As him who conquer'd France!
Richard! the splendid child of her
    Whose beauty was romance.*

---

* Edward the Black Prince married his father's cousin *Joan*,
(called from her beauty) the Fair Maid of Kent, being the only
surviving child of Edmund Earl of Kent. Though she had been
twice married before, the Prince, passionately loving her, married
her; and by her had two sons—*Edward*, born at Angouleme, who
died at seven years of age; and *Richard*, born at Bordeaux, who
became King Richard II. "He was," says Sir Richard Baker,
"the goodliest personage of all the kings that had been since the
Conquest; tall of stature, of straight and strong limbs, fair and
amiable of countenance, and such an one as might well be the son

13.
Richard! the Lord's anointed king!
The nation's lawful prince!
Percy might set him wondering,
But could not him convince

14.
That Wrong was Right, however Right
Might dabble with the Wrong;
He could not blind his own eye-sight,
His conscience was too strong.

15.
But when Earl Percy and his son,
And brother Worcester too,
Regretted all that they had done,
And would the same undo—

16.
Then he afforded ready help
To their endeavouring;
The dogs of war let loose to yelp.
He halloo'd to the gathering.*

17.
" Non-intervention" 's mean pretence
He could not carry out ;
An honest man of common sense,
He must be " cold," or " hot."

---

of a most beautiful mother." Both parents were descended from
King Edward I., as thus—

Eleanor of Castille=King Edward I.=Margaret of France,
who at the age of 18 married
King Edward II.   Edward when above 60, and
had
King Edward III.   Edmund Earl of Kent, who
was the father of

The Black Prince..............=Joan the Fair Maid of Kent.

King Richard II., born at Bordeaux, A.D. 1366.

* The two brothers, Henry Percy of *Northumberland* and
Thomas Percy of *Worcester*, had both been created *Earls* by the
obliging and somewhat womanlike Richard ; and yet they both
fell away from him to the usurper, by whom *Worcester* was made
king's lieutenant of Wales, and also governor of the young Prince
Henry and his household ; from whom also they both at length
revolted for the causes already shown.

18.

Lord Bardolph and his men of war
Many forc'd marches made ;
But neither Percy nor Glendôr
Their banners yet displayed.

19.

Northumberland himself lay sick
At Berwick-upon-Tweed ;
The Welsh Prince might have been more quick
To keep the terms agreed.

20.

But Hotspur's uncle, Worcester's Earl,
Was marching hard and fast,
Hotspur to meet, and to unfurl
Their common flag in haste.

21.

Too eager with these firebrands
To make the bold attack,
Without the other high commands
Their eagerness to back.

22.

Hotspur—with Worcester and allies,
In all twelve thousand men—
Transported with impatience hies
To Shrewsbury's fatal plain.*

23.

An equal number Henry brought,
Together with his son,
Well pleased to see a battle fought,
And how it might be won.

---

* Camden, in his account of Shropshire, thus notices the battle
of Shrewsbury :—" When divers of the nobility conspired against
Henry IV. with a purpose to advance Edmund Mortimer, Earl of
March, to the crown, as the undoubtful and right heir, whose father
(Roger Mortimer) King Richard II. had also declared heir apparent, then Sir Henry Percy, called *Hotspur*, addressed himself to
give the assault to Shrewsbury. But upon a sudden, all their designs were dashed. For the king, with speedy marches, was upon
his back. To whom yet the young Hotspur, with courageous reso-
lution, gave battle : and, after a long and doubtful fight, wherein
the Scottishmen, which followed him, showed much manly valour
(when the Earl of Worcester, his uncle, and the Earl of Dunbar
were taken) : he, despairing of victory, ran undaunted upon his
own death, amidst the thickest of his enemies. Of this battle, the
place is yet called BATTLE-FIELD : and there, the king afterwards
builded a chapel, and settled two priests to pray for the souls of
them who were there slain."

24.

The arch usurper show'd his skill.
Like one who plays at chess ;
Glory—he gave a bitter smile :
Honor—he honor'd less.

25.

Like ancient Ahab, *Lancaster*
Put others in his guise,
That they might stand the shock of war
While he the danger flies.*

26.

And, as *Benhadad* gave command
To single *Ahab* out,
So *Lancaster* bade all his hands
To bend on *Hotspur's* route.

27.

To every captain of the host.
And to *ten knights* then made.
" Hotspur must die at any cost,"
The kingly traitor said.

28.

" Care not for either small or great.
Only mad *Hotspur* slay ;
He is the god-of-war's own mate,
Him dead, we have the day."†

* The historian *Speed* writes thus : " The lord *Percy* and earl *Douglas* (than whom the wide world had not two braver champions) instead of spending themselves upon the multitude, set the point of their hopes on killing the king, as in whose person they were sure ten thousand fell. For this cause, they most furiously rushed forward with spears and swords ; but the Earl of Dunbar [a refugee Scot] discovering their purpose, drew the king from the place, which he had chosen to make good, and thereby, in likelihood, for that present, saved his life ; for the Standard Royal was overthrown, and (among other valiant men), the Earl of Stafford, Sir Walter Blunt the king's knight, and the standard bearer himself was slain : such was the fury of these sudden thunderbolts. That day, the *Douglas* slew with his own hands *three* in the king's coat armour, though *Boetius* yet saw a *fourth.* Sure it is, that many of the subjects thought the king was slain, and, *according to Walsingham*, many thousands ran out of the field. But the slaughter could not be small on both sides, the archers shooting so continually, and the men at arms doing their utmost for about the space of three whole hours."

† See 1 Kings, xxii., 30, 31.—" On the king's side," according to the respective historians *Speed* and *Baker*, "were slain, besides the Earl of Stafford, ten new knights, whose names are recorded as—1, Sir Hugh Shirley; 2, Sir John Clifton; 3, Sir John Cocayne; 4, Sir Nicholas Gawsell; 5. Sir Walter Blunt; 6, Sir John Calverly; 7, Sir John Massie; 8, Sir Hugh Mortimer;

29.

'Twas on the twenty-first July,
Fourteen hundred and three,
The seventh day, called Saturday,
This battle was to be.

30.

Hot-headed Percy led the horse,
Spur-ring to use his might,
As though upon his single force
Depended all the fight.

31.

He gave direction to *begin*,
And, to his order true,
The arrow which *first* left the string
From *Hotspur's* bowmen flew.*

32.

In solid mass the spearmen stood,
The marrow of the power,
Prepar'd to second as they could
The arrow's deadly shower.

33.

Hotspur, upon his frantic steed,
Scorning lieutenants' aid,
Rush'd here and there with spirit-speed,
Quicker to be obey'd.

34.

At length to his own body guard,
And from his saddle-throne,
While his excited charger rear'd,
He thunder'd—" Follow on !

9, Sir Robert Gawsell; 10, Sir Thomas Wendesley; all being
knighted that morning, and fighting for their spurs about the
standard. There were also slain many esquires, and gentlemen,
and about one thousand and five hundred common soldiers, besides
three thousand sorely wounded."—" On the other part," adds the
same *Lancastrian* account, " omitting that *Second Mars*, the lord
Percy, who drew a ruin after him suitable to his spirit and great-
ness, there fell most of the esquires and gentlemen of Cheshire, to
the number of two hundred, and about five thousand common
soldiers. This battle was stricken near to Shrewsbury, upon a
Saturday, the one and twentieth of July, and the Eve of St. Mary
Magdalen."—[Of course the *executed prisoners*, taken *in* and *after*
battle, are to be reckoned among " killed " on this occasion.]
     * " We will content ourselves," says *Speed*, " with the know-
ledge of God's part in this day's work, *who gave the garland to the
king, though the first arrows flew from the Percie's archers.*"

35.

"St. George for England! and for heaven
St. Michael, he will fight ;
Although to man no grace be given,
Yet—God defend the Right ! "

36.

Forward they followed, like a cloud
In summer, pouring rain,
Whose dashing drops with fog enshroud
The suddenly drench'd plain.

37.

Mighty the charge, yet madly done,
Wanting prospective plan ;
As though the battle might be won
Merely by horse and man.

38.

The king's troops stagger'd, and gave way,
And many yielded breath ;
Amid confusion and dismay,
They tumbled into death.

39.

But the king's well prepar'd reserve,
Their lesson having learn'd,
Re-acted in a hollow curve,
And on their victim turn'd.

40.

Fresh to the ground, him they surround,
As though a beast of prey ;
A tiger, from whose dreadful bound
They fain would turn away.

41.

Devoted numbers hemm'd him in,
Despite of all they fear'd ;
While through the back, and with a grin,
One *wretch* his body spear'd.

42.

Thus fall, not seldom, by the base,
The bravest of mankind ;
The choice—the noble—thus give place
To some ill-gotten hind ! *

---

* Shakespeare, in his play of "Henry IV." (first part), com-
placently, but most absurdly, gives the credit of slaying *Hotspur*
to the young Henry Prince of Wales, at that time a mere youth of
16 or 17 years old, and little likely to measure swords with one like
Hotspur, in the full force of youthful manhood. Besides which,

43.

None dar'd to boast, in all that host,
  Of that assassin-blow,
Which from behind some coward tost,
  And laid the warrior low.

44.

Lord Bardolph saw the fatal sweep,
  And shouted to his train—
" Form up, three deep; close order keep!
  Charge! Wermigey men!

45.

" Rescue Hotspur, living or dead—
  Let no man dare retire :
Look where ye tread, beware his head,
  Think of his father's ire.

46.

" On to the front, and bear the brunt
  Of a false king's array;
On to the front, 'tis a Royal hunt—
  Like bloodhounds, stand at bay!"

47.

Steady and stern, the captains burn
  To teach the daring feat;
Steady and stern, the soldiers learn
  To do the deed complete.

48.

So surely as one wounded man
  Fell in the foremost rank,
So quickly from the rear one ran
  To occupy the blank.

49.

Wary and watchful, one small force,
  With only sword and dirk,
Prepar'd to seize the noble corse,
  And ably did their work.

50.

Speedily fled with Hotspur dead
  To a far lonely spot;
In a cool shade his body laid,
  Although not there to rot.

---

had this been the case, historians who, like Hume, Baker, Speed,
Dugdale, and Camden, profess to relate the most accurate accounts,
would not coincide to ignore such an event, and to record that the
greatest hero of the day *"fell by an unknown hand."*

51.

Again the Baron's voice on high
Spoke like the clarion clear :
" Forward ! Reserves of cavalry !
All forward from the rear !

52.

" Trot—canter—gallop—horse brigade !
Trot—canter—gallop—fly !
Away, rankriders ! * Tilt the blade ! †
Kill the false king, or die !

53.

" Heedless of ward, your blows afford
Like flashing rays of light ;
Let every man bestow his sword
With all his art and might.

54.

" Leap, like the leopard, when he makes
A spring upon his prey ;
Ride over lance and battle-axe—
Do your best deeds to-day ! "‡

---

* " Rankriders,"—the ancient name for light cavalry, troopers,
or dragoons, trained to charge and fight in concert and good order.
† " Tilt the blade,"—give point, or thrust with a good aim.
‡ This splendid feat of arms, which the French cuirassier cavalry
did *not* dare attempt at Waterloo, *was* both dared and done by the
British light cavalry (the 3rd Bombay Europeans) of the *late*
" Honorable East India Company" 's army, in their celebrated
charge over infantry in square, at Kooshab, in Persia, as may be
seen *represented* in the " Illustrated London News" (vol. xxx.,
pp. 383, 384) of the 25th April, 1857, where it is also related by a
Bengal officer, in proof of what horsemen, well led, can do, even
against a fence of bayonets. After describing the formation of the
Persian square as excellent, and untouched by artillery, he proceeds
thus : " When *Forbes*, who commanded the regiment, gave the
order to charge, he and his adjutant, young *Moore*, placed themselves in front of the 6th troop, which was the one directly opposite
the nearest face of the square. The other *Moore, Malcolmson,* and
Spens came the least thing behind, riding knee to knee, with spurs
in the horses' flanks. After them rushed the dark troopers of the
3rd. In spite of steel, fire and bullets, they tore down upon the
nearest face of the devoted square. As they approached, *Forbes*
was shot through the thigh, and *Spens'* horse was wounded. But
unheeding, they swept onward. The barrier once broken, and the
entrance once made, in and through it poured the avenging troopers.
On and over everything they rode, till getting clear out, they re-
formed on the other side, and swept back, a second wave of ruin.
Out of five hundred Persian soldiers of the 1st Regular Regiment
of Fars, who composed the fated square, only twenty escaped to
tell the tale of destruction."

55.

The cunning crafty Lancaster
  Knew when to shift his ground ;
So when the foe thought he was there,
  An *effigy* they found.

56.

A *Royal effigy* was found,
  And yet a better man
To yield his life for him was bound,
  While he made off and ran.

57.

Full many a hero-man that day,
  Full many a hero-horse,
Before that night all stiffen'd lay,
  A carcase, or a corse.

58.

'Tis said the king slew thirty foes
  (Poor wretches !) in the fight—
While at the hide and blink with those
  Of whom he fear'd the might.

59.

Hotspur and Douglas he eschew'd—
  (No hand to hand with them !)
Concentrate others there he could,
  And yet save his own fame.

60.

Brave Douglas, Percy's prisoner,
  Lately become his friend,
Had joined him in his rash career,
  And closely would attend.

61.

Though gifted with a chief's command,
  Too forward to display
The prowess of his single hand,
  He slighted his high sway.

62.

Too eager to avenge the dead,
  He mingled in the throng ;
And speedily, a captive made,
  Was by them borne along.

63.

A horse-fall and a wounded eye
  Occasion'd the disgrace ;
But the sad *cause*, which we espy,
  Was —*being out of place !*

64.
A chieftain ought to be the " Head "
To sway the " Limbs " to fight ;
He should direct, and be obey'd
By their effective might.*

65.
Courage alone cannot atone
For lack of discipline ;
Rulers should rule, and subjects own
The rulers' "right divine."

66.
On shipboard, if the captain's word
Be slighted on the deck,
Or no commander's voice be heard,
The vessel goes to wreck.

67.
Or if the captain, like a sprite,
About the rigging fly,
Tack, steer, load guns, the vessel fight,
As though no help were by—

68.
What could evene from such wild scheme
But ruin and defeat ?
Who could of conquest ever dream ?
Who could avoid his fate ?

---

* " We shall scarcely find," says Hume, "any battle in those
ages, where the shock was more terrible and more constant. *Henry*
exposed his person in the thickest of the fight. *His gallant son*,
whose military achievements were afterwards so renowned, and
who here performed his noviciate in arms, signalized himself in his
father's steps, and even a wound which he received in the face,
with an arrow, could not oblige him to quit the field. *Percy* supported that fame which he had won in many a bloody combat :
and *Douglas*, his ancient enemy, and now his friend, still appeared
his rival amidst the horrors and confusion of the day. This nobleman performed feats of valor which are almost incredible : He
seemed determined that the king of England should that day fall
by his arm : He fought him all over the field of battle : and, as
Henry, either to elude the attacks of the enemy upon his person,
or to encourage his own men, by the belief of his presence everywhere, *had accoutred several captains in the royal garb*, the sword
of Douglas rendered this honour fatal to many." To which Sir
Richard Baker adds that " the king was once unhorsed by Douglas,
who in his presence slew *Sir Walter Blunt*, with divers others,
that day in all things *attired like the king*. For which exploit,
Douglas, being after, *by the fall of his horse*, taken prisoner, was,
by the king's command, carefully attended, and without ransom,
set at liberty."

69.

So, of one (skill'd to make all yield)
Clear head and courage cool,
The need was taught at " Battle-Field,"
And learn'd at " Shrewsbury school."

70.

Percy and Douglas, when in arms,
And *face to face* array,
Like champions upon equal terms
Their prowess did display.

71.

Percy and Douglas *side by side*,
In double might, allow'd
The victory from both to glide,
And to the traitor bow'd.

72.

Oh! had they conquer'd, that foul blot,
That stain to England's page,
The " Roses " faction, had been not,
That curs'd the future age.

73.

Had they shed *Henry Fourth* his blood,
No *Henry Eighth* had been,
That woe to lovely womanhood,
That ogre of all sin.

74.

Had they, with Worcester, and the rest,
And Hotspur's father too,
And Owen Glendôr, plann'd their best,
Like Bardolph and his few,—

75.

Together, all together fought,
In a grand unison,
Restrain'd impatience as they ought,
The victory had been won.

76.

But Hotspur's men and Hotspur's friends,
In terrified dismay,
Instead of trying an amends,
Fled panic-struck away.*

---

* " While the armies were contending in this furious manner,"
writes David Hume, " *the death of Percy, by an unknown hand*,
decided the victory, and the royalists prevailed." To which may
be added the words of John Speed: "That which gave an end to
this woful work was the death of *Hotspur*, who, riding at the head

77.

Not Bardolph, with his gallant band,
And gallant bearing too,
Avail'd to bring them to a stand;
They fled as madmen do.

78.

Unaided in his warlike feat,
Un-seconded by all,
He sought to cover their retreat
By a *third* trumpet call.

79.

His own men, foot and cavalry,
Sped to his gathering.
Alternately to fight and fly,
But orderly retiring.

80.

The royal host in haste pursued,
Prince Harry had command,
But Bardolph his retreat made good,
And reach'd Northumberland.

81.

" Northumberland " his tardy aid
Was bringing to his son :
" Too late! too late! " Lord Bardolph said,
" The battle's lost and won.

82.

" Earl Douglas is a prisoner ;
Worcester, I doubt, will die ;
Hotspur no more will lead the flower
Of northern chivalry.

83.

" The bloody despot has the day,
For, after Hotspur's fall,
His followers have fled away,
Cravens and cowards all.

84.

" Mean men will now a merit make
Of bending to Lancaster,
And strive both you and me to take
And sell to that slave-master.

of the battle, in defiance of danger and death, was, *by an unknown hand*, suddenly killed : with whose fall (as if the whole army had had but one heart), the courages of all the others fell into their feet, which now altogether they trusted to."

85.

" Combine our forces, make a stand
  Upon some vantage ground,
Where we have odds at our command,
  And staunchest friends abound.

86.

" This chance is past—his may not last,
  For from the battle plain
The tyrant may himself be chas'd,
  Or, better still, be slain."

87.

Percy was wary—though aghast—
  Himself was not committed ;
His sky, indeed, was overcast,
  But the king might be cheated.

88.

He would dissemble—" *that the fight*
  Was Hotspur's and not his ;
He might have brought up all his might,
  He still had large supplies."

89.

Not yet, however, could he trust
  Even this policy :
Bardolph's advice follow he must—
  Prepare to fight and die.

90.

" To Werkworth castle let us wend,"
  Earl Percy then replies ;
" At Werkworth castle, good my friend,
  Await extremities."

91.

Meanwhile, the astute Lancaster
  Counts up his loss and gain ;
Each *ransomable* prisoner,
  Each partisan that's slain.

92.

The Earl of Worcester he secur'd,
  And, full of rage and spite,
For all the terror he'd endur'd,
  Condemn'd to death that night.

93.

Douglas he treated as a Scot ;
  But on the Monday morn
He order'd Hotspur to be sought
  And from his green grave torn.

94.

This enemy in death he dreads,
  And round his body stalks ;
The ghastly form he first *beheads*,
  Then *quarters*, like an ox !*

95.

So truculent, so barbarous,
  So cowardly are some,
Who yet both high and prosperous
  And honor'd to become !

96.

Not yet content, this savage king,
  This fiend in human guise,
The several pieces gathering,
  In separate parcels ties.

97.

Each parcel to some city sends,
  To show what he would do
To all who would not be his friends,
  To each who was a foe.

98.

Yet Hotspur's wife was Henry's blood,
  And sister of a prince,
The rightful king ; Hotspur too could
  His own kinship evince.

99.

Reason the more, you may be sure,
  Why Hotspur and his league
Should vanish before Henry's power,
  By force or by intrigue.

100.

These orgies done, to York he went,
  Thence orders (forward north)
To Percy and his friend he sent
  From Werkworth to come forth.

---

* "After this victory, the king caused public thanks to be given
to God, and then caused the Earl of Worcester to be beheaded, and
many others of that rebellion to be drawn, hanged, and quartered,
and their heads placed on London bridge."—(*Baker's Chronicle.*)
" Hotspur's body had been buried," says the historian *Speed*, " but
upon other advice, the king caused it to be drawn out of the grave,
beheaded, quartered, and the parts sent into divers cities of the
kingdom."

101.

" Safe conduct, pardon—on submission—
Should be their free award ;
But prompt must they be in decision,
Or none would he afford."

102.

The friends agreed to take the terms,
Though they might end in death ;
Whatever from a traitor comes,
Could warrant little faith.

103.

Still they risk'd all upon his word—
Earl Percy's plea was ready,
And though enrag'd by all he heard,
His mien was calm and steady.

104.

Not so Lord Bardolph, whom the king
Stung with a victor's vaunt ;
Disdain—grief—wrath up towering,
Thus answer'd he the taunt :—

105.

" Lord king ! the sword of conquest wins
A plenitude of right,
Against which right itself but sins,
If hopelessly it fight.

106.

" Thou hast the day, yet can thy sway
Not long last over men,
If like a butcher thou dost slay
A second time the slain.

107.

" Hotspur fought valiantly and died,
And men lament his fate,
But thou insanely didst divide
His body in thy hate.

108.

" Horror, nor terror, thou wilt sow
In every Englishman ;
In thy own mind shall " terror " grow,
When thy own deeds it scan.

109.

" Butcher us all, yet we who fall
Shall multiply in others,
Who will avenge, and proudly call
Thy victims their dead brothers.

110.

" Serpents of anguish and remorse
   Shall fasten on thy throat,
For every dead man's quarter'd corse
   On whom now thou dost gloat.

111.

" Thy superfluities of naught
   Both God and man disgust ;
He who to-day is over-haught
   To-morrow bites the dust.

112.

" Here, at death's door, I fear no more
   Ten thousand kings like thee,
Than ocean waves alarm the shore
   Which they lash endlessly.

113.

" Fill up the measure of thy crimes—
   Heaven waits the holocaust ;
Mankind shall live in after times,
   When *thou* art *dead* and *lost !* "

114.

Thus found the Baron's wrath a vent,
   Thus burst his bitterness ;
A withering look therewith he sent
   At the usurper's face.

115.

Astounded at the daring words,
   A prisoner's withal ;
Words which no flatterer records
   His wincing soul appal.

116.

Conviction smote the hard king's heart,
   The sword blow of a truth
Quell'd his high anger with the smart,
   And turn'd revenge to ruth.

117.

'T were e'en good policy, he knew,
   To show some lenity ;
And thus, as mingled motives grew,
   He spoke forbearingly.

118.

" De Wernigey ! the skill which thou
   Didst show upon the field
Demands a commendation now
   When thou art forc'd to yield.

12

119.

" Serve on my side instead of those
Disputers of the throne ;
More worthy they to be thy foes
Than he who wears the crown.

120.

" Thy life—thy lordship—and thy love
I value at their due ;
Accept a pardon, and then prove
If " Henry " can be true."

121.

So to Northumberland he made
A similar award,
Thinking—through Hotspur's shiver'd shade—
His heart enough was gor'd.*

122.

Percy, in silent anguish, bow'd—
His bitterness he quell'd—
Passions too violent would crowd
To be in words detail'd.

123.

His grief intense, his boundless scorn,
His hatred of the man ;
His self reproach that he had borne
A share in the rash plan

124.

Of humbling HIM to raise up *him*
Who sat upon his throne ;
His consciousness of a fool's crime,
Which nothing could atone.

125.

The dread bereavement he endur'd,
The fear of even more,
The silence of his tongue secur'd,
He mask'd the pangs he bore.

---

* "The king, having humbled the Earl of Northumberland, in such sort as you have heard, looks again upon him with an eye of compassion and favor, *not without a secret respect to his own safety ;* and he had little appetite to augment enemies, but to allay them rather ; whereas, by this gracious usage of that Earl, he now thinks those north parts sufficiently secured. The full restitution to the Earl was made in the Parliament holden at London, about the midst of January, 1404, *when the king obtained an unusual tax, or subsidy, of which* (that it might not be drawn into example) *no record nor writing was suffered to remain.*"—(History of England by John Speed.)

126.

The conclave parted, ill at ease,
Both those who won and lost ;
Even good fortune cannot please,
Bought at so dear a cost.

10th August, 1403.

Day of St. Lawrence.

WERMIGEY.

PART V.

HOME—AND ITS SYMPATHIES.

A.D. 1403.

"Then are they glad, because they are at rest, and He bringeth them unto the Haven, where they would be."—DAVID, *Ps.* cvii. 30.

1.
There is a thought—a word—a wish—
Most dear to those who roam ;
The young—the old—the poor—the rich --
All sigh for " Home, sweet Home ! "

2.
Home is the goal of Human Hope—
The treasure-house of Love ;
Earth-spurning Faith itself looks up
Only to Home above!

3.
Home is a bright-eyed fairy spot
Amid the darkest gloom ;
It glimmers, though we have it not,
Like a lamp in a tomb !

4.
Home is the comfort, and the rest
And refuge of the soul ;
Home is the bosom we love best,
Which *can* and *will* console—

5.
Whether of parent, or of child,
Of brother, or of sister.
Or that one worthy to be styl'd
The wife—the self-sinister.

6.

Whether it be in humble cot,
Whether in princely hall,
Home is the kernel of the nut,
Home is the all-in-all.

7.

Of all the tongues of all mankind,
Of all the lands I've seen,
There is but one in which I find
The *word* and *thing* I mean.

8.

'T is thou, my father-mother land,
'Tis thou the white-cliff'd isle;
In nature small, in glory grand,
The world's HOME thou art still!

9.

Lord Bardolph sought his "home" once more,
His water-moated hall;
His gallant-looking castle tower,
His rounded rampart wall.

10.

All things familiar, far and near,
Associated too
With *beings* dear secreted there
By those *things* from his view.

11.

With smiling pleasure—sighing pain—
Hopeful, yet fearful doubt—
He wearies to see all again,
He longs to find them out.

12.

Rivers and churches, farms and towns,
In order due pass by,
And then appear the breezy downs
In front of Wermigey.

13.

The dear old Priory at hand,
Ever at watch and ward,
If any grief befal the land,
Some comfort to afford.

14.

The hill-guard sentries all alert—
(Old faces, with some scar on)
In soldier duties less expert
Than glad to see the Baron.

15.

Delighted to watch some return
From Shrewsbury's " Battle-Field,"
Eager to learn whom they must mourn,
What comrades have been kill'd ?

16.

Earnest in talk, as on they walk,
Indulg'd with liberty ;
No martinet was there to baulk
Their curiosity.

17.

Over the water, on the banks,
Women and children stood ;
The castle-guard's saluting ranks
Still nearest to the flood.

18.

The happy children, happy wives,
Esteem'd that day and night
The happiest of all their lives,
And yet, *not happy quite !*

19.

Orphans and widows were in tears.
Bewailing Shrewsbury's fight ;
And Happiness itself has fears
When seeing such a sight.

20.

There was a chapel in the square,
Where those who mourn'd could kneel ;
The castle chaplain daily there
Pray'd with a holy zeal.

21.

There would the fortunate and blest,
From their abounding store,
A heavenly treasury invest,
By giving to the poor.

22.

There came bereavéd sorrowers,
Of God to ask relief,
And to become the borrowers
Of them who had no grief.

23.

There came the generous to give,
The grateful to repay ;
And all a blessing to receive
Before they went away.

24.

Such was the Baron's family,
His people rich and poor ;
They practis'd heavenlike sympathy,
And heaven came to their door.

25.

What comfort he himself enjoy'd,
What exquisite delight,
To find all zealously employed,
From the serf to the knight.*

26.

To feel his own, his chosen " vine," †
Wreathing around his frame,
With her two tendrils who combine
To call him by his name.

---

* Concerning the knights of Wermigey. In addition to the
" large possessions " taken from the Dano-English Baron *Turchil*,
or *Turchetil*, and granted to the Norman-French Baron *Hermer
de Ferrers*, the Barony of Wermigey went on increasing its terri-
torial property, first, by the lawless seizures or invasions of *Hermer*,
and then by annexation through marriage alliance. In the 7th
and 8th of Henry II., *Richard* de Wermigey, son of *Hermer* de
Ferrers, was found to hold 14½ *knights' fees in capite*, and 2 *of the
old fealment* of Hugh Bigod. And, in the 45th of Edward III.
(when John Lord Bardolph died, August 3rd), there were belonging to the honor and manor of Wermigey about 20 *knights' fees*.
Besides which, and a long list of other manors, there were Clopton,
in Suffolk ; Burgh, Hekinton, Cathorp, &c., in Lincolnshire ; and
Stake Bardolph, in Nottinghamshire, as part of this lord's Barony
of Shelford, to which, as it is said, there were 29 *knights' fees belonging*. (See *Parkin*.)--In the history of the Battle of Agincourt,
and the expedition of Henry V. into France, in 1415 (twelve years
after the Battle of Shrewsbury), by Sir Harris Nicholas, K.H., and
in the roll of the men-at-arms of the English army, the retinue of
Sir William Phelip (created " Lord Bardolph " as the husband of
the last lord's younger daughter Joanna) is stated to have consisted
of *viii. Lances* and *xxix. Archers ;* and the names of seven knights
are thus recorded : 1, Thomas Holwyscout ; 2, William Gode ;
3, John Barnard ; 4, Thomas Poley ; 5, Robert Hemnale ; 6, Jacob
Denys ; 7, William Kemston ; of whom *Thomas Poley* was of an
ancient family of that name, of Boxted Hall, in Suffolk ; and in the
church of Boxted parish is the following epitaph on one of his descendants : " Under this marble, is buried, awaiting the second
coming of our Lord, *Sir John Poley* of *Wrongey*, in the county of
Norfolk, *knight*, second son, and at length heir of *Thomas Poley ;*
a man famous for bravery in arms, and, for military skill, to be
reckoned among the first commanders. Satisfied with his share of
life and fame, he sank placidly to sleep in the Lord, having passed
his eightieth year. He died at his manor in *Wrongey*, in the year
of our Lord 1638."

† " Thy wife as the vine upon thy house."—Psalm cxxviii. 3.

27.

" Husband! or Father! " each one said,
" What bliss to meet so well!
After such agonizing dread—
Oh! 't is unspeakable! "

28.

It seem'd as though it were not so—
It might be yet a dream,
In which they knew not what to do—
Weep—laugh—lament—or scream.

29.

Then, in default of that relief,
The want came rushing by—
After their mid-night watch of grief,
To sink asleep in joy.

30.

Their hearts went gazing through their eyes
And listening through their ears,
At him, the burden of their sighs,
The answer to their prayers.

31.

His glaive—his reins—his saddle-gear—
His soil'd accoutrements—
His glorious charger standing near,
Looking at *him* askance.

32.

The wife—the children—noted all—
The very ground he trod;
But, when they heard him some one call,*
Oh! how they worshipp'd God!

33.

The lord was in his hall again—
His brave companions there—
The knights—the squires—and the men,
With sword, and bow, and spear.

34.

All life—all safety—all delight—
All kindliness and glee;
The armour glitter was so bright,
It did them good to see.

35.

A mute, unmingled thankfulness
Pervaded all the four;
A timid kiss, a tight embrace,
Said all they could, and more.

---

* " The voice of my beloved!"—CANTICLES. ii. 8. 11; v., 2.

36.

For trivial talk there seem'd no use,
 With so much inward joy ;
And *speech* its power will refuse
 When *song* we should employ.

37.

There was a favorite household HOUND,
 With silver-collar'd throat ;
At each, in turn, he made a bound,
 And bark'd a joyous note.

38.

Not unrequited was his love,
 Not spurn'd, nor yet unheeded ;
Each brim-full heart was glad to prove
 The little kindness needed.

39.

There was a HARP but newly strung,
 At which no harper sate,
And yet, inside, sweet songs were sung,
 Clear voices did vibrate.

40.

Such mystic music murmur'd round,
 That things inanimate
Appear'd to echo at each sound,
 Each thought to modulate.

41.

There was an ornamental GLASS
 That vision'd loveliness ;
And now it sparkled every face
 With rays of happiness.

42.

The CURTAINS hanging in the shade
 Beside the window light,
Like sleeping infancy betrayed
 That they dream'd of delight !

43.

A frowning HELM, a grim CUIRASS,
 A deadly HARQUEBUS,
All smil'd ! for so it comes to pass
 All things take part with us.

44.

It is *not* that the implements
 Or harnessings of war
Themselves engage the sentiments
 Of the brave or the fair ;

45.

It is that they *belong to those*
Who are our own heart's core,
And may be *safeguards from the foes*
Of whom we dread the power.

46.

It is the *mind* those things invests
With its own inward tint,
And then the bliss within our breasts
Takes from those things a hint.

47.

Pregnant with pleasure, Nature teems
To give new pleasures birth ;
Innate effulgence bursts and beams
Through all the pores of earth.

48.

As though that substance which supports
This superficial frame
Were weary of those four escorts
Which we the seasons name ;

49.

And were about to cast disguise,
And show that brilliant Being,
Which nature's matter underlies
In an eternal spring ! *

50.

'T is thus the kind Eternal grants
Some foretaste of that future
When we shall not need this world's wants,
But dwell with Him in rapture !

51.

So they were happy ! In that space,
That given point of time,
Converg'd a focus of God's grace,
And was it not sublime ?

52.

Complete contentment, perfect peace,
No thought, no wish for more ;
Only a thorough thankfulness,
Renew'd from hour to hour.

---

* "A new heaven, and a new earth wherein dwelleth righteousness."—Isaiah, lxv., 17 ; lxvi., 22. 2 Peter, iii., 12, 13. Rev., xxi., 1.——"No night there."—Rev., xxii., 4.——"Mortality swallowed up of life."—2 Cor., v., 4.

53.

A brimming cup, for each to sup,
　And say, " How good the store ! "
Life's present held life's future up,
　It had *prospective* power.

54.

The Great Provider, could He fail
　Ever to be the same ?
Could He do else but all things well,
　And make them praise His name ?

55.

'T is well and wise not to devise
　What evils *may* evene ;
'T is well and wise while this day flies
　To keep our sky serene ;

56.

To chase all gloom away from home
　Save that sweet solemn peace
Which, like some moon-lit holy dome,
　Draws angels to the place ;*

57.

To gild—to paint—to deck each room
　In which we have to live,
As bees, who roam, bring honey comb
　And honey to the hive ;

58.

To rest in love's benignities,
　To dwell upon his charms,
To feed upon his charities,
　And shield him from alarms ;

59.

To help *each other* in that way,
　For that which we afford
Of cheer or comfort will one day
　Become our own reward.

*　*　*　*　*　*

---

* Those who have seen and felt the effect of moonlight *inside*
Der Dom at Cologne, or Canterbury Cathedral, or King's College
Chapel at Cambridge, or the like " holy domes," can understand
how near heaven the many *outside* people may be, without knowing it, or attaining to it.

60.

The summer pass'd—the autumn came—
The winter breezes blew—
The season when the olden Fame
Said this fair world was new.*

61.

Between the first day and the last
Of our September time,
Creation's bells went *pealing* fast,
Though now they only *chime*.

62.

For now " Creation " waxes tame,
And wearied of its roll ;
And, sick with human guilt and shame,
'T will soon begin to *toll*.†

63.

In the year fourteen hundred three,
Striving the world to cheer,
It still blew soft at Wermigey—
Many were happy there.

64.

The Baron and the Baroness,
With their young family,
Enjoy'd what now is call'd " recess,"
Their autumn holiday.

65.

Leaving the castle's *etiquette*,
They sought the manor hall,
Far from the martial sounds and state,
And yet not out of call.

---

* The Hebrew month Tizri (September—October) was reckoned by the Jews the first month of the year, the first day of which was the Feast of Trumpets, which then commemorated the Creation, " when the morning stars sang together, and all the sons of God shouted for joy."—(See Exodus, xxxiv., 22. Psalm, xix ; lxxxi. Job, xxxviii., 7.)——The modern Jews also have a notion that on this day God judges all men, who pass before Him in review, as a flock before the shepherd ; a notion not without foundation, for it anticipates that " harvest time " when Christ shall come again to judge the world, with His " reapers," the angels.—See Matthew, xiii., 30, 39.

† "The end of all things is at hand."—(See 1 Peter, iv., 7. 2 Peter, iii., 10.)——"The heavens shall vanish away like smoke."—(See Isaiah, li., 6.)

66.

In that home-haven, husband, wife,
  Parent and petted child,
Escaping courtly laws and life,
  Delighted to run wild.

67.

The lord could doff his lordly ways,
  The soldier his attire ;
The mother with her children plays,
  The rustics own the squire.

68.

The wood—the water—the decoy—
  The cover for the game ;
The park—the garden—they enjoy,
  And " all belongs to them."

69.

The happy girls, in rosy health,
  Were at that favor'd age
When childhood reaps its precious wealth
  And needs no check too sage.

70.

The one had thirteen winters seen,
  The other summers twelve ;
They still might gambol on the green
  And in a *parterre* delve.*

71.

" Father and mother ! " they exclaim'd,
  " This is the fall of year ;
Look at the misletoe we 've gain'd,
  Look at the acorns here.

72.

" We 'll keep the one for Christmas fun,
  The corn-cups we will share ;
But now we come with you to run
  And race, you darling pair.

73.

" Hark ! how the oaks echo the strokes
  Of yonder woodman's axe :
And hear the rooks reading their books ;
  Oh ! what a din it makes ! "

---

* Of these two sisters, *Anna* the elder was born 24th June, 1389
(13 Richard II.), and *Joanna* the younger was born 12th November, 1390 (14 Richard II.), and they were now at the autumn of
1403.—(See Lib. de Legibus Antiquis, pref. p. 152.)

74.
Sweet are the simple joys of youth,
 None can with them compare;
And, with such play-mate parents both,
 Were *they* not happy there ?

75.
For in their pleasure and their play
 The genial parents join'd,
Enhancing childhood's ecstasy
 With their own wit refin'd.

76.
" Dear Avice ! " said the sire and spouse
 To her who sought his arm,
When wearied with the wild carouse,
 Although it was a balm.

77.
" Dear Avice ! see those charming chits,
 Those fair young buds of ours !
On them how pleasantly life sits,
 Rejoicing in youth's powers.

78.
" Fond—fresh—and free—as they might be
 If born before the Fall,
And this were Eden's sanctuary,
 A home celestial !

79.
" Like the three flowers on our shield,
 Except the *wanting one*,
Which Heaven chooses not to yield,
 Our death-demanded " son " !*

80.
" Like two clear stars that gem the sky
 Our wedded sky of blue—
Instead of being *you* and *I*,
 They shine a *double you !* "

81.
The shield, or " field," or banner flag,
 Of Bardolph was of blue,
And three gold cinqfoils on the rag
 Gave a bright light thereto.

---

* See the large seal of *Thomas* Lord Bardolph as engraved in
the notes appended to Part II., where *one cinqfoil* is almost
obliterated.

82.

The *blue* they deem'd the heavenly *bliss*,
  Balming a wedded pair ;
The *flowers*, like stars in heaven's abyss,
  The blooming children were.

83.

Thus did they choose the shield to use,
  And mutually say—
" How pleasant thus to walk and muse,
  And pass the time away !

84.

" How pleasant, with the merry morn
  And children to be gay ;
How pleasant, when the sun went down,
  Their sadder thoughts to say ! "

85.

For at that sadder eventide,
  Close to each other plac'd,
Would they sit talking side by side,
  With arm in arm enlac'd.

86.

Then would the Baron oft revert
  To his lost son and heir,
And plaintively unheal the hurt
  They still could scarcely bear.

87.

" Dear Avice ! that belovéd boy,
  Part both of you and me,
Who was the centre of our joy,
  Whom God took dreadfully—

88.

" Who would have made our age's aid,
  Thine and the girls' resource,
Should I be number'd with the dead
  Before thy finish'd course.

89.

" Dear Avice ! that belovéd boy
  Still cries with a loud voice—
Why were we parted—why, oh why,
  Without our own free choice ?

90.

" Why were we given to be blest,
  Only such pain to prove ?
So closely press'd for death to wrest
  One from the other's love ?

91.

" Truly, the Providence of God
  Endures no reasoning ;
As in a cloud He doth enshroud
  His every proceeding.

92.

" Amid the bounties of our lot,
  Some other good we crave ;
Whatever blessings we have got,
  One more we wish to have !

93.

" Vast is our soul ! vast its desires !
  Vast as the sky we see ;
O vast, too vast, its hungry fires
  For our felicity.

94.

" Temper'd by trial and by time,
  We scarcely learn to live,
Ere time and trial, grief or crime,
  Only let smoke survive.

95.

" Without reflection and restraints,
  Without a guiding hand ;
Without God's teaching providence,
  We never understand—

96.

" Never regard that " still small voice,"
  The chastener of our hearts—
Never make His will our free choice,
  Till taught by sorrow's arts."

97.

Thus would they ponder till distrest,
  Then sigh, and wish, and pray—
And each demand to be carest,
  To cheer sad thoughts away.

98.

Yet so it was, not without cause,
  They were thus melancholy ;
There are in nature secret laws
  Which stir our sympathy.

99.

Often some old oppression comes
  To warn us of a new ;
The past foreshadows future glooms.
  And now it was so too.

14

100.
The Lady Agnes Mortimer,
Lord Bardolph's widow'd mother,
(To whom they were indebted for
Their knowledge of each other)

101.
Was dying—if not dead—and they
Were call'd from their retreat
By the alarm—anxiety—
And filial heart-beat—

102.
To take her benedictory
Farewell! and feel again
The sharp truth of that old story,
The fruit of man's first sin!

103.
The snapping of that earliest tie,
A mother's interest,
Which all the way from infancy
Makes even bad men blest.

104.
Ah! there are no tears can assuage
The grief men owe their mothers,
Though they might often check that rage
Which murders those of others!

105.
O God! all men are bretheren,
Yet, through the spite of hell,
Mothers must, of their own children
The fratricides bewail!

106.
Man—that is of a woman born—
Hath but short time to live—
Yet do they so each other scorn,
And make each other grieve.

107.
Dependent on the softest care
Of woman's soft control,
Still they go on to do and dare
What wounds her to the soul.

108.
Proud   selfish   brutal—diabolic
Sons scoff at sacred ties—
While mothers, like the church catholic,
Lavish their charities.

109.

O woman fair—O woman dear—
What would mankind become
Without thy never ceasing care
To *woman*-ize man's home ?

110.

Sad victim of one fatal fault
That drove us from the sky,
Before the damnable assault
Of our Arch-Enemy—

111.

How studiously dost thou repair
The ruin of that breach ;
How diligently run to share
Man's troubles in thy reach !

112.

How perseveringly engage
All through this poor life-time,
From infant days to helpless age
To lessen pain and crime !

113.

Sweet mother—sister—daughter—wife—
Our antidotes of sorrow—
Sweeteners of all things in this life,
Past—present—and to-morrow—

114.

Man thinks *his* intellect is clear,
Man thinks *his* rights divine,
But, from the cradle to the bier,
Sweet woman ! *he* is *thine!*

115.

Not property so much to prize
As chiefly to lament
Both love's and labor's enterprize
Dash'd by dis-appointment !

116.

Not property whereof to boast,
Excepting now and then,
When, like a jewel miss'd and lost,
One cheers them up again.

117.

Lord Bardolph, at his mother's bier,
Conceded her to God,
As though himself her guardian were
And she become his ward.

118.
His own superior so long made,
  Now lying there to crave,
As she once plac'd *him* in his bed,
  To place *her* in a grave!

119.
O dark surprise—O dread idea—
  Of one so long-lov'd gone—
No more to cherish and revere,
  But only to bemoan.

120.
Although the Parent of them both
  Had settled the right time
For them to part, however loth,
  However hard for *him*—

121.
Unnumber'd tender memories
  Threw him upon the rack,
Till like a child again he cries,
  " O give my mother back ! "

122.
But no reply, to cry, or sigh,
  Awaits his anxious ear,
Nor meets his unbelieving eye
  That death may not be there.

123.
Conviction—reason—common sense—
  All prove reality ;
And yet the heart, on some pretence,
  Thinks it a falsity.

124.
That horrible impassive state,
  That stillness full of awe,
Of those we talk'd with but so late,
  Yet hear us now no more !

125.
All bountiful as God may be,
  In things we care not for,
So ruthlessly refuses He
  Our dead ones to restore.

126.
And yet He acts impartially—
  He ever was the same
Towards those He watch'd most tenderly,
  He alter'd not for them.

127.

There fell a pious son, of old,
On his dead father's neck—
(Although a prince of wealth untold)
As if his heart would break.*

128.

There never was a *son* like him,
There never was a *man*,
Except God's SON, more free from crime,
And yet he wept in vain.

129.

Joseph, like Jesus, cried aloud,
" O leave me not alone ! " †
But each had answer from his God,
" Come thou to me, my son ! " ‡

130.

The only consolation left
To us beneath the sky,
Is that, those of whom we're bereft
May meet us by and bye.‖

131.

So Bardolph thought, and fondly hoped
To meet again each " friend,"
And carried, in his bosom coop'd,
This hope unto the end.

---

* " And Joseph fell upon his father's face, and wept upon him,
and kissed him."—Genesis, l., 1.
† " Eli ! Eli ! lama sabacthani ! "—Matthew, xxvii., 46.
‡ " Out of Egypt, have I called my son."—Matthew, ii., 15.—
" He that overcometh, shall inherit all things ; and I will be his
God, and he shall be my son."—Rev., xxi., 7.
‖ " And Israel said unto Joseph, Behold I die ! but God shall
be with you, and bring you *again to the land of your fathers,*—even
the Almighty who shall *help* thee—and *bless* thee unto the utmost
bound of the *everlasting hills !*"—Genesis, xlviii., 21 ; xlix., 25, 26.

Little happiness, it would appear, could the Lady
Agnes Poinings-Bardolph-Mortimer have enjoyed in
her second nuptials with *Sir Thomas Mortimer*, whom
Dugdale misnomers Sir *Roger* Mortimer, and whose
lineage, the preface-writer of *Liber de Legibus Antiquis* says, " has not been satisfactorily determined."
However, the following is ascertained : Of all the
five branches of the Mortimer family, who settled
respectively at *Wigmore* castle, *Ricard's* castle, *Attilburgh, Cherke,* and *Chelmersh,* it is clear that he be-
longed to the family at *Attilburgh,* in Norfolk ; and
that he was the third son of Sir Constantine Mortimer
(who was in the retinue of John de Warren, Earl of
Surrey, and died 12th Nov., 1334,) and grandson of
Sir William Mortimer (a ward of Earl Warren), who,
in 1285, impleaded the Prior of Shouldham next Wermigey, for the advowson of Stamford church, and set
forth his pedigree on that occasion : and who was summoned to Parliament as a Baron in 1296, and being
in France that same year, was taken prisoner, and
died in Paris. As for Sir Thomas Mortimer, his
grandson, who married Lady Agnes Bardolph, he
was impeached of high treason [in the Parliament
begun at Westminster, Monday, 15th Sept., 1397
(21 Richard II.), and from thence adjourned 29th
Sept. to Shrewsbury] by Edward Earl of Rutland
(whose brother Richard of Coningsburg married Ann
Mortimer, heiress of England) and other lords appel-
lant, and by the commons of the realm, by reason of
his being then a *fugitive.* It had been alleged against
him that, having been made privy to the plot of
Thomas Duke of Gloster, and Richard Earl of Arundel, he, together with Thomas Earl of Warwick,
assented to their traitorous designs ; and that these
four, of one accord, had assembled a vast force at
Haringeye, in Finchley, co. Middlesex, on the 13th
November, 1387 ; and that, in the following year, at
Huntingdon, on Thursday, 14th May, 1388, the same
four proposed to march against the king, wherever
he might be, in order to depose him from his royal
estate, and take the crown into their custody. It
was, therefore, ordained by the king, with the assent
of the states of Parliament, that proclamation be
made, as well in the realm of England, as in the land
of Ireland, warning him to appear before the king
wherever he might be, within three months after the
21th September; and, in case of default, to be ad-
judged a traitor, with his adherents. Briefs were

sent by the Chancellor of England to Roger Mortimer, Earl of March, the king's lieutenant in Ireland,
as well as to every sheriff in England, to seize his
person, and all his possessions were declared forfeited
to the king from the 13th November, 1387 (11 Richard II.). All the proceedings of this Parliament
were annulled in the first Parliament of Henry IV.
(6th October, 1399) ; but it is doubtful if Sir Thomas
survived to that time; but, it being known that his
place of retreat was in Ireland, and that he had been
a leader of the rebels in that island, (and opposed to
King Richard, in whose company was his own step-
son, Lord Bardolph,) in Ireland most probably he
died. In any case, he was deceased prior to the 9th
of June, 1403 (4 Henry IV.), as the will of Agnes
Lady Bardolph, " *widow of Sir Thomas Mortimer*," is
of that date, and made during a residence in the
dwelling house of Richard de Vere, Earl of Oxford,
then a minor, (son of King Richard's friend and
favorite, the Duke of Ireland,) in the parish of St.
Augustine Papey, in the city of London. In this
same year 1403, and on the 13th March, the Lady
Agnes had obtained the king's license to go on a
pilgrimage to Rome and Cologne, with twelve servants and their horses, and all accoutrements fit for
such a journey; but failing health precluded the
fulfilment of this intention. Her will, dated on the
9th June, was proved on the 15th October. One of
its provisions directs her body to be buried in the
priory of the Holy Trinity without Aldgate; and
another contains an appointment of *Henry Earl of
Northumberland* and of her son *Thomas Lord Bardolph*
to be supervisors of the same.

WERMIGEY.

PART VI.

MICHAELMAS DEVOTIONS,
A.D. 1404.

" Thou, that hearest prayer—unto thee shall all flesh come!"—
DAVID, Psalm lxv., 2.
" Call upon me in the time of trouble—so will I hear thee, and
thou shalt praise me."—DAVID, Psalm l., 15.

1.
A year pass'd by, while wounded men
   And wounded spirits groan ;
Cursing the dread usurper's reign,
   Whom their hearts could not own.

2.
Their bodies heal—their spirits rise—
   They meditate—they hope
Again their all to jeopardize,
   Again with him to cope.

3.
At Wermigey, that heavy lull
   Which home-born sorrow brings,
And tends to disengage the soul
   From outward earthly things—

4.
Was only yielding to the wiles
   Of true love and religion,
And beauty's persevering smiles,
   And cheerful youth's contagion—

5.
And he, the husband and the sire,
   Had open'd all his heart
To all the bliss he could desire
   And all they could impart—

15

6.

When lo ! like clouds which after rain
Just stop to note effect,
Then send their torrents down again,
So troubles now re-act.

7.

One day, when harvest work was o'er,
And all enjoyed repose,
In the year fourteen hundred four,
The last long storm arose.

8.

A knight—four mounted men-at-arms—
Stood at the hill-guard gate ;
A bugle sounding five alarms,
Proclaim'd they there did wait.

9.

The warder challeng'd—" Who came there ? "
The answer was—" A friend ! "
Urgent despatches he did bear,
Northumberland did send.

10.

Northumberland—Archbishop Scroope—
The Earl of Nottingham—
Lords Hastings—Falconbridge—did group
With other men of name,

11.

To sue Lord Bardolph them to join
In a new tentative,
To set the right king on the throne,
Their common relative,

12.

Young Mortimer; first, as a right
Due from them all to him ;
And then because the art, the spite,
The avarice, the crime,

13.

Of Lancaster, offended all,
Endanger'd all, and made
The lives of all seem criminal
As well as full of dread.*

---

* " In the Parliament held this year (1404) at *Coventry*, called
the *lack-learning Parliament* (Parliamentum indoctorum), *in order
to supply the king's wants*, a Bill was exhibited *against the temporalities of the clergy*. But, by the courage of the Archbishop of
Canterbury, the motion vanished to nothing, but to the infamous

14.

" One day," wrote Percy, " I shall die
By that atrocious king—
Victim both of his tyranny
And my own paltering.

15.

" The which, unless I can retrieve
And guard my young grandson,
What right, indeed, have I to live
At the usurper's boon? "

16.

So wrote Earl Percy with the rest
To Bardolph ; and his brother
Follow'd up, in their interest,
Their counsels, with this other.

17.

" Brother and chief ! 't is my belief
The king has *no remorse*,
But watches, like a lurking thief,
Where he may filch a purse.

18.

" A traitor, and a tyrant too,
Reckless of rich or needy ;
A *Janus* man, of double view,
Both truculent and greedy.

---

memory of the attempters."— " Twice, after this, however, between
Christmas (1404) and Palm Sunday (1405), did the king again as-
semble the states, once at *London*, and then at *St. Albans*, for the
cause of *money*, but with much distaste,—the peers of the land rising from the last session thereof meanly contented, as it well appeared not long after, though to the enterprisers' ruin. *Thomas
Mowbray*, Earl Marshall, one of the chief men which disliked the
carriage of public matters, draws *Richard le Scrope*, Archbishop of
York, into a conspiracy, in full hope that *Henry Percy*, Earl of
Northumberland, the *Lord Bardolf*, the citizens of York, and the
common people, would assist their cause."—" The Earl of *Westmoreland*, hearing of this attempt, wherein the Earl Marshal and
the Archbishop were leaders of the people, gathers a force to encounter them ; but perceiving himself too feeble, *he betakes himself
to fraud ;* and, *feigning to like the quarrel*, got both into his power,
and presented them as an acceptable oblation to the king, who,
about Whitsuntide (1405), comes to York, where *(albeit the Earl
of Westmoreland had promised them their lives,)* as well the Archbishop as the Earl Marshal, *were beheaded.* But the next year, the
Pope excommunicated all such as had a hand in putting the Archbishop to death."—*(History of England by John Speed.)*

19.

" Thou hast not answer'd to his hope
In courtier-like beseeking,
Since he did dash the martyr cup
From thy lips rashly speaking.

20.

" Jealous, and conscious of his foes,
Before them he may start ;
Northumberland, he too well knows,
Must hate him in his heart.

21.

" He cannot but perceive and feel
How insecure his crown,
Which any day Dame Fortune's wheel
May trundle upside down.

22.

" Surely the peerage of the land
Must be degenerate ;
Or, like King John, his stern command
Would soon be out of date !

23.

" There is a story of this king,
His father, John of Gaunt,
That he was *a foreign changeling*,
Not the royal infant ! *

---

* " William Wickham, Bishop of Winchester, who had risen
from the humblest origin by his merit, was the object of *an invete-
rate envy.* When he was Lord Treasurer of England, and the
king (Edward III.) required a supply of money, it was answered
that he needed no other supply than to *call his Treasurer to account.*
This blow struck deep upon the Bishop, for he was presently
charged to give account for eleven hundred and ninety-six thousand (1196000) pounds ; and, whilst he was preparing his account,
all his temporalities, on the importunity of *John of Gaunt,* were
seized into the king's hands, and given to the Prince of Wales, and
himself forbidden to come within twenty miles of the court. This
being the case, he dismissed his train, and sent abroad *copies of his
account,* if it might be received ; but in this he was hindered *by the
working of John of Gaunt,* upon this ground (as was thought) :—
Queen *Philippa,* upon her deathbed, by way of confession, told
Wickham that *John of Gaunt* was not the offspring of King Edward, but a supposititious son ; for, when she gave birth to a
daughter at *Ghent,* knowing how desirous the king was to have a
son, she exchanged that *daughter* with a *Dutch* woman for a *boy*
born at the same time ! Thus much she confessed, and withal
made the Bishop swear that, if *John of Gaunt* should at any time
attempt the crown, or that rightfully it should devolve upon him,
that then he should discover this matter unto the king and council.
Afterward, the queen being dead, and the Bishop finding *John of*

24.

" That Queen Philippa did confess,
    When on her dying bed,
She could not leave this world in peace,
    Without this statement made.

25.

" She had a *daughter*, not a son—
    (Ye heavens, who overlook!)
And for this daughter of her own
    Another's offspring took!

26.

" Simply because Edward the Third
    She knew preferr'd a *boy;*
And that he might be vex'd she fear'd,
    And wish'd to give him joy.

27.

" Wickham, Bishop of Winchester,
    She caus'd to take an oath,
That should this boy the throne come near,
    He would declare the truth.

28.

" Both *Winchester* and *Gaunt* are dead,
    And now, for aught we know,
Some Dutchman's grandson in his stead
    Works England's bitter woe!

29.

" No wonder he detests the blood
    He knows is not his own;
Dutchman, or *devil*, little good
    Does he upon the throne.*

Gaunt too much aspiring, secretly told him this relation and adjura-
tion of his supposed mother, advising him not to seek higher than
a private state, or else he was bound by oath to make it known to
all the world. The duke, it is certain, bore a mortal grudge to the
Bishop, who however enjoyed a quiet life afterwards, and died in
the 4th year of Henry IV. (1403), at the age of eighty years, and
lieth buried, in a monument of his own making, in the church of
St. Swithin's, in Winchester."—(See *Baker's Chronicle*, Henry IV.)

    * Sir William Bardolf's *good opinion* of the usurper, as a money
appropriator, was soon to be attested by events. On the attainder
of his brother Thomas Lord Bardolf,—1. The honor and manor
of Wermigey, together with Stow-Bardolph, North Rungton, and
Fareswell Manor in Fincham, *were granted*, by Henry IV., *to his
own brother Thomas Beaufort*, Earl of Dorset, Duke of Exeter,
who died without issue 27th December, 1426, when they reverted

30.

" In any case, *the rightful heir
Of Richard is alive*—
King Edmund, the young Mortimer,
Is Bardolph's relative.

31.

" In any case, Elizabeth,
His aunt, is Hotspur's wife ;
Dead Hotspur's widow languisheth
And groaneth out her life.

32.

" In any case, their orphan son,
Young Harry Percy, claims
Guardianship and protection
From the usurper's aims.

33.

" All England calls upon her chiefs
To rectify this wrong ;
And for what are baronial fiefs
But to check kings too strong ?

34.

" How much more when that king is naught—
A wholesale murderer—
In England's orb a great black blot,
Causing that orb to err ! "

35.

So reason'd William Bardolph, and
Too weightily indeed
His reasons seconded the band
With whom he so agreed.

36.

What a responsibility
Do those incur who give
Advice ! but more especially
To those they may bereave—

---

to the king.—II. *Item :* The manors of Shelford and Stoke-Bar-
dolf in Nottinghamshire, the manor of Halloughton in Leicester-
shire, and Burling in Sussex *(where Thomas Lord Bardolph was
born)*, were granted, by letters patent of King Henry IV., bearing
date 10th August, 1405, *to his most dear consort Joan, Queen of
England*, to hold for the term of her natural life, in part of the de-
duction of ten thousand marks annually by him granted to his same
consort, who died at Havering in the Bower (Essex) on the 10th
July, 1437 (15 Henry VI.).

37.

God knows to what extent! How sure
They should be of the right,
The *true*—the *whole* right—but no more
Or less than is right quite!" *

38.

Lord Bardolph chew'd the bitter cud
Until the hour of sleep;
And heavily he slept, but could
No rest or quiet reap.

39.

His thoughts throughout the day before
Pursued him in his dreams;
*His lovely wife, as dead, he saw;
He heard his children's screams.*

40.

*He saw the butcher Lancaster,
With crimson color'd hands,
And overcome by the nightmare,
Himself a prisoner stands.*

41.

With violent emotion woke,
He turn'd him in his bed;
His heart—his limbs—his body shook,
And thus he murmuréd—

---

* " Sir William Bardolph was the third of the three children of
William and Agnes, Lord and Lady Bardolph; of which children
the eldest appears to have died an infant,—Sir Thomas (Lord Bar-
dolph) being the second child. In the ensuing reign of Henry V.,
Sir William Bardolph was Lieutenant of the Captain of Calais,
Richard Earl of Warwick. He died without issue on Sunday the
Feast of St. James the Apostle, 25th July, 1423 (1 Henry VI.),
seized, for the term of his life, of the manor called *Kingeshall*, in
Clopton, Suffolk, together with the advowson of the church of
Irbach, belonging to the same manor, worth 40s. annually, held of
the lord the king in chief by fealty, and the render of one *pair of
gilt spurs*, price 6d., for all services, according to an inquisition
taken at Woodbridge, 15th September, 1423; which properties
then came to his two nieces (daughters of his deceased brother
Thomas), *Anna*, aged 34, widow of Sir William Clifford, and
Joanna, aged 33, wife of Sir William Phelip. In 1401, he presented Richard Swayne to the church of St. Edmund, at Caistor.
His widow Joan remarried to Richard Snelling, who, in the 3rd
Henry VI., released this manor for an annuity to the Ladies Anne
Clifford and Joan Phelip. Sir William Bardolph was also possessed
of the manors of Quinbergh, Cantele, Strumpeshagh, in Norfolk,
with all their appurtenances and advowsons, which likewise came
to his two nieces aforesaid."—*Lib. de L. A.*, p. 183.

42.

" O Avice dear—art thou still here,
My wife, my only one?
O why didst thou so pale appear,
And why was I undone? "

43.

" What ails my love? why so distress'd? "
The wife responded him;
" Compose thee to thy needful rest,
Think of some holy hymn.

44.

" Take a sweet kiss—restore the same—
Fold me in thy embrace—
And let us pray, in Jesu's name,
O God protect and bless!

45.

" No harm can come but by his doom,
Our souls to Him are dear;
In earth, in heaven, He makes our home,
Him only let us fear.

46.

" Reign in thy home—be here content—
Keep far away from strife;
Blight not the blessings he has lent,
Thy children and thy wife! "

47.

The soothing words—the soothing tones—
The soft reproach he felt—
Though he could only utter groans,
In love his spirit knelt.

48.

In doating thought, he worshipp'd her
With wordless gratitude;
And in the tresses of her hair
Both tears and kisses strew'd.

49.

For her he made believe repose,
Vex'd for her broken sleep;
Resolv'd, whatever were his woes,
Them in his breast to keep.

50.

The man who after duty yearns
Fears to distress a friend;
Fears for his own most cherish'd ones,
Not his own fate or end.

51.

On *her* good soul, the due reward
    Of her own love and faith,
In peace and sleep was richly pour'd
    With each succeeding breath.

52.

No so the harass'd man of care,
    No rest in heart and brain ;
He sought, indeed, her peace to share,
    But sought it all in vain.

53.

The dead of night brought no respite
    From the dread vision given ;
The future still baffled his sight—
    With doubt his mind was riven.

54.

At length he rose ere break of day
    From wearisome unrest,
Before the sound of *reveillée*,
    Which slumberers detest.

55.

The night-watch waited the alarm
    With longing and delight,
To lay aside the ponderous arm
    They carried through the night.

56.

The Baron mounted up the tower
    To view the eastern sky ;
It was not quite the rising hour,
    But coming bye and bye.

57.

The warder struck the morning bell.
    The trumpeter stood up,*
Preparing with a blast to tell
    The eye of day to ope.

58.

The clarion call'd the fogs to clear,
    They shiver'd with the shock ;
When, like a smile after a tear,
    A gleam of sunshine broke.

---

* Possibly the son, or grandson, of that trumpeter, "*John Bokingham*," to whom the last Lord William Bardolph granted a strip of land at Market Downham, in 1380.—(See the Notes to Part II. and William Lord Bardolph's seal.)

59.

The glowing sun, scaring night glooms,
  Rose like a ball of blood ;
[As when a conquering hero comes,
  Daring to be withstood—

60.

Scaling a fort with sword in hand,
  To plant a red cross flag,
And shouting out the fierce command
  Another down to drag !]

61.

The Baron mark'd the wondrous glare,
  Thus conquering the night,
And, rising out of his despair,
  Thrill'd at the cheering sight.

62.

" God of Creation ! " he exclaim'd,
  " Thou art *indeed* the Morn !
O let *Thy Spirit* thus proclaim'd
  On my dark spirit dawn !

63.

" Let heavenly hope my gloom dispel,
  Grant me to have success ;
Thou Light of Light Invisible !
  Allay my soul's distress.

64.

" Guide me, in all things, while I stay
  In this world's banishment ;
Save me from earning day by day
  Sin's dreadful punishment.

65.

" Go with me where I ought to go,
  While I have life and breath ;
Do with me what Thou hast to do,
  But save me after death ! "

66.

His eyes the waving standard fix,
  That flag of " blue and gold " ;
The flag-staff was a crucifix,
  He took it in his hold.

67.

He kiss'd the cross—he made the sign—
  He whisper'd " Jesu Christ !
On earth—in heaven—Redeemer mine—
  Preceptor—King—and Priest ! "

THE CASTLE-TOWER BANNER.

"His eyes the waving standard fix,
    That flag of blue and gold ;
The flag-staff was a crucifix,
    He took it in his hold."

                    "Wermigey," Part VI., v. 66.

68.

This was his morning orison—
This was his private prayer—
But with an added benison
"That all around might share ! "

69.

The eastward town of busy men—
The hill-guard on the west—
The northward priory, and then
The southern water waste.

70.

To post new sentries, the reliefs
Were pacing to and fro ;
Little they thought their last of chiefs
Was praying for them too !

71.

One word he to the warder spoke,
And then repair'd below ;
And gather'd up an ample cloak,
All " blue and gold " I trow.

72.

" Boatman, ahoy ! " the warder cried
To one upon the " ley,"
In a small skiff, the " brig " beside,
" Look where the bargemen be ! " *

73.

" Bid them prepare the Baron's barge
To seek the priory ;
Order the scullers, next in charge,
For duty instantly ! "

74.

The men were muster'd in short space,
Each with his oar uplift ;
The mooring at the landing place
Ready to cast adrift.

75.

Soon stood the Baron on the brink,
Soon stept into the boat ;
The oars beneath the water sink,
And smoothly fast they float.

---

* On each side of the West-Brig road, the low lands, once under
wa'r, are still called in history " le ley," and are still styled by the
villagers " the leys," and the only way they have of accounting for
the term is that, before the great drainage, the fish lay there in
comparatively shallow water, where they might always be caught
in abundance.

76.

Soon reach'd the quiet convent shell
Of cloisters all around ;
The chapel bell now tinkled well,
The early matins sound.

77.

From here and there, to morning prayer,
Hurried each hooded friar ;
While, thinking only of his care,
The Baron sought the Prior.

78.

Good *Hugh de Fincham* in those days
The priory controll'd ;
And twenty years of prayer and praise
Had not yet made him old.*

79.

" Father ! I come in lowly mood,"
The Baron meekly said,
" For thee to intercede with God
For His Almighty aid.

---

* *Tanner* calls this a Priory of Black Canons, built by William,
son of Reginald de Warren, in the time of King Richard I., or
King John, to the honor of the Virgin Mary, the Holy Cross, and
St. John the Evangelist. It was united A.D. 1468 to the Priory
of Pentney, and from that time was looked upon as a cell thereto.
It was valued in the 26th Henry VIII. at £35 9s. 1d. In the 4th
Edward VI. this small priory was settled upon the Bishoprick of
Norwich. The following is *Blomefield's*, or rather his continuator
(*Parkin*)'s list of the Priors of Wormegay :

1. Ralph, 18 Henry III.
2. Nicholas, 14 Edward I.
3. John de Boylond, presented by Hugh Lord
   Bardolph, A.D. 1300.
4. Nicholas de Elme, A.D. 1302.
5. Robert de Craneworthe, A.D. 1315.
6. John de Cauntely, A.D. 1330.
7. Simon de Leveringham, A.D. 1349.
8. Michael de Thornham.
9. Robert de Fordham, A.D. 1370.
10. Hugo de Fincham, A.D. 1383.
11. Hugo de Watlyngton, A.D. 1416.
12. Robert Walsyngham, A.D. 1447.
13. John Methelwold, A.D. 1461.

And in the year 1468 this priory was (in consequence of poverty
occasioned by floods and the loss of the ancient patrons, the Bardolphs) annexed, with all its members and appurtenances, to the
adjoining priory of Pentney.

80.

" Deep in my soul an anguish broods,
Which needs a mighty power,
To be cast out, ere it corrodes
My mind and manhood more.

81.

" My grandsire bore *St. Michael's* name,*
(A soldier-saint, they say)
And church bells all around proclaim
It is *St. Michael's* day.

82.

" Order a special noon-day mass,
Our troops to sanctify,
That, at each church, a special grace
Be sought of the Most High.

83.

" Myself and brother will attend—
He at the *Western* shrine ;
And you and I our steps will bend
To *Michael's* the divine.†

84.

" Soldiers, of all men, most diverge
From Christian sanctity,
Therefore need they the more to urge
Their vows of piety."

85.

" 'T is well, my son," rejoin'd the prior,
" 'T is well thou hast the thought
To stand upon a standard higher
Than any earthly lot.

86.

" God's blessing go with thee this day !
Allay thy bosom's strife !
Whate'er befal thee in the way
Unto Eternal Life.

87.

" Issue thy orders to the knights—
Gladly will we adhere ;
I will direct the solemn rites—
Heaven grant us Heaven's cheer ! "

---

* His mother's father was *Michael* Lord Poynings.
† Wermigey church is dedicated to Saint Michael, or Mi-cha-el, which signifies *Who* (is) *as God*. "The Great Prince" (Daniel, xii., 1) who, " with his angels, made war in heaven against the devil and his angels, whom they cast out."—Revelations, xii., 7-9.

88.

The Baron took the Prior's hand,
And held it in his own—
" Good father! still one more demand—
Pray for me all alone !

89.

" As though to-day my time were come
To quit this tent of clay,
To meet my everlasting doom—
Pray for me, father, pray.

90.

" Lo! on my knee, I wait the word
In thy commission given,
To certify me from the Lord
That I have peace with heaven!"

91.

"Son!" said the Prior solemnly,
" The Searcher of all Hearts
Grant that in thee all sin may die
And frustrate Satan's arts!

92.

" Grant thee conviction of this grace,
Through his atoning blood,
Who did fulfil all righteousness,
To bring thee near to God!

93.

" Grant thee the gracious *sight* to see,
The gracious *sense* to know,
The gracious *skill* and *strength* to be
Like him who lov'd thee so!

94.

" Accept the trials of thy faith,
The labors of thy love!
Fear not the day or deed of death—
He waits for thee above !"

95.

No more he said, but each hand laid
Over the suppliant's brow,
In token of the blessing shed
Upon that suppliant now.

96.

They parted then to meet again
With all convenient speed,
Attended by the warrior train,
As by them was agreed.

97.

The Baron's second-in-command
(His brother had this claim)
The Westbrig church (St. Botolph) mann'd—
" Sir William " was the same.*

---

* The Rectory of Wermigey was in the Priors of Wermigey,—
but the Rectors of Westbrig were independent, and are thus
chronicled by Blomefield (or Parkin) :—

1. Richer de Fulius, A.D. 1190, presented by Hugh, Prior of
Castleacre.
2. Sebastian de Florentino, A.D. 1230.
3. In the 13th of Edward I. (A.D. 1285), an exchange was made,
on William Lord Bardolph's grant of North Birlingham church
(St. Peter's), and this advowson was given to that lord.
4. William de Speeteshale, A.D. 1300, presented by Hugh Lord
Bardolph.
5. Ponwardus de Montmartin, A.D. 1313, by Alice de Hannonia,
Countess of Norfolk.
6. Peter de Monte Martini, A.D. 1314, by Thomas Lord Bardolph.
7. John le Blakeshale, A.D. 1316, by same.
8. Nicholas Cannard, A.D. 1321, by same.
9. Thomas de Cailly, of Wroxham, A.D. 1323, by Thomas Lord
Bardolph, of Wirmegaye, to whom he was chaplain.
10. Gilbert Quintin de Hethill, A.D. 1327, by Thomas Lord
Bardolph. This Rector is also called Parsona de Tottenhill. He
died in the 9th of Edward III.
11. William de Culchith, A.D. 1336.
12. John de Westacre, A.D. 1339, by John Lord Bardolph.
13. Simon Norreys, A.D. 1349, by same.
14. Lawrence Mareshall, of Tirington, A.D. 1349, by same.
15. Robert de Barrowe, A.D. 1367, by Queen Philippa, by grant
from the king, as guardian to *William*, son and heir of *John* Lord
Bardolph, taxed at 17 marks.
16. Thomas Stoner, A.D. 1368, by Queen Philippa.
17. John de Weston, A.D. 1371, by the king.
18. John Walton, A.D. 1397, by Sir Thomas Mortimer.
19. Roger Baret, A.D. 1403, by *Thomas* Lord Bardolph, but
subsequently resigned, and probably in disgust on account of the
sad fate of his noble patron, and distaste of his successor.
20. William Alyngton, A.D. 1411, by *Thomas Beaufort*, knight,
admiral and chancellor of England, half-brother to Henry IV.,
Duke of Exeter, *a wooden effigy of whom was found in this church
by the present writer A.D.* 1861.
21. On the 18th July, 1416, this church was appropriated, by
the same *Thomas Beaufort*, to the Priory of Wirmegay, to be
served by one of the canons, with which Priory it came to be appropriated to Pentney Abbey, then to the Bishop of Norwich, then
to Queen Elizabeth, and finally to the Bishop of Ely, who now
pays the Vicar *twelve pounds yearly* out of the church revenue.
The two churches themselves, now most mean, were once much
nobler structures. In 1847, the writer, when repairing Wermigey,
discovered *relics* of departed grandeur; and while this book is
printing, Westbrig chancel is repairing, and still more numerous
tokens of ancient glory come to light.

98.

Both East and West, the churches hold
A simultaneous prayer,
With every man alternate told
For duty—here—or there.

99.

The *Prior* and the *Rector* each
Had his respective staff
Of aids to sing, and pray, and preach,
In these poor souls' behalf.

100.

To the far East of Wermigcy
Baron and Prior mov'd,
With all their forces on the way,
In order as behov'd.

101.

Past the Guildhall and Market Cross
The martial column trod,
With measur'd step o'er moor and moss,
Towards the House of God.

102.

Beside the solid altar stone
The Prior sought his place,
Eyeing the crosses five thereon,
And bowing down his face.*

103.

Canons and choristers also,
Each found his proper post,
Ready to join their voices to
Those of the Heavenly Host.

104.

Before the sacred symbols stood
Lord Bardolph—sad in mind—
Though both in look and attitude
Like a brave man resign'd.

105.

The *knights* behind the Baron pair'd,
The *men-at-arms* beyond,
As many as at castle-guard
Were not on duty bound.

---

* This ancient relic with its five crosses is now a portion of the
chancel pavement.

106.

The spears of these—the swords of those—
Were at their usual rest,
Piously taken (I suppose)
With themselves to be blest.

107.

Either the soldier's work is right
When wrought in a good cause,
Or dimly burns religion's light,
And we mistake its laws.

108.

St. Michael the Archangel fought
In heaven a fight divine,
Therefore both hearts and "arms" they brought
To brave St. Michael's shrine.

109.

To pray that they in righteous fray
Might have St. Michael's aid,
And with good angels in the way,
Never to be afraid.*

110.

The mass began—the incense rose—
The tuneful tones accord—
Affrighted fly men's mortal foes
When Christians seek their Lord.

111.

The *men-at-arms* their weapons lift
With both hands to present,
As if to tender God's own gift,
Which they acknowledge lent.

112.

From *knightly scabbards* leap the swords
And on each shoulder slope,
While every voice declar'd the words
Of Christian Faith and Hope.

113.

Creed and *Te Deum* loud they sang,
And nobly stemm'd despair ;
The walls and roof with praises rang,
And then they knelt in *prayer.*

---

* "O everlasting God! who hast ordained and constituted the
services of Angels and Men, in a wonderful order—mercifully grant
that as Thy Holy Angels alway do Thee service in Heaven, so, by
Thy appointment, they may succour and defend us on Earth—
through Jesus Christ our Lord. *Amen.*"—(The collect for the day
of St. Michael and All Angels.)

111.

They heard an *exhortation* spoke
As by a brother's voice—
And duty urg'd so that it woke
Devotion—as of choice.

115.

They heard a *benediction* said,
And deep repentance vow'd ;
And, in a silence like the dead,
Each gave his soul to God.

116.

Uprising—not asham'd of tears—
Shed by the best of men—
Sabres return'd—and grounded spears
Responded *their* Amen !

117.

And now they breath'd the open air—
And now for nothing mourn'd—
But light of step, and heart, and care,
To quarters they return'd.

118.

The day soon clos'd—and all repos'd—
Curtain'd by comfort given—
Fearless of all to be disclos'd
In future—this side heaven.

PART VII.

EASTER FAREWELLS,
A.D. 1405.

"Lo! I am with you alway, even to the end of the world."—
Matthew, xxviii., 20.

1.

'T is true : true lovers do *not* part,
    They *never* separate ;
The presence is where is the heart,
    That is the Clock of Fate.

2.

Its pulses move the magic hands
    Which prove the life within it ;
LOVE strikes the hour ; and when it stands,
    TRUTH points that mournful minute !

3.

The Eye of Faith reflects a beam
    Which other eyes avert ;
Jacob saw angels in his dream,
    When his eyelids were shut.*

4.

Faith is Love's ready telescope,
    Which views the spirit-world,
And thence derives the glorious Hope,
    Whereby Fear's flag is furl'd.

5.

'T is true, indeed, that Love desires
    All that belongs to Love,
But Absence does not put out fires
    Kindled in heaven above.

---

* Genesis, xxviii., 10—22.

6.

The Saviour did not leave his friends
By being lost to sight;
He never ceas'd to make amends
By His *hovering* Spirit.

7.

Five hundred proto-martyr saints
Were sad to see Him go,
But wasted not in vain complaints
Their own short time below.*

8.

Rememb'ring those sweet words he said—
" *Wherever two or three*
Call upon Me, their Risen Head,
With them I there will be"— †

9.

Soon to the Temple they adjourn,
Continually to praise; ‡
And so with all, who love and mourn,
Continually He STAYS. §

10.

" Always *with* you—always *with* you,"
His voice condoling cries;
" Always *for* you—always *for* you,"
His pleading Spirit sighs.||

*   *   *   *

11.

The month was March, the spring of year,
When, since the world began,
Princes who must go forth to war
Open a new campaign.¶

12.

In winter drills and discipline
The troops are now exact;
And almost anxious to begin
The parts they have to act.

---

* Acts, i., 9—11; and 1 Cor., xv., 6.   † Matt., xviii., 20.
‡ Luke, xxiv., 50—53.   § John, xiv., 16—18, and 23.
|| Romans, viii., 26, 27, 34.
¶ The month of March, or *Mars*, the god of war, became the
first month of the year, not only with the Romans, but also with
the Jews. —See 2 Sam., xi., 1 : "The time when kings go forth to
battle."—See also Exod., xii., 1—2.

13.

As chargers, rein'd and saddle-bound,
  Enthroning valiant men,
With swords and scabbards girded round,
  Are eager for the plain;

14.

So men themselves, in strength and pride,
  With duties to fulfil,
Desire also to have tried
  Their courage and their skill.

15.

Mankind are restless, even when
  They have no work on hand;
How needful to be under, then,
  Some good and wise command.

16.

Some cannot rule—some must obey—
  All cannot be the head;
The happiest and best are they
  Who follow duty's lead.

17.

Lord Bardolph was prepar'd to join
  A daring enterprize;
With Percy—Mowbray—Scroope, again
  The chance of war he tries.

18.

Such was his " duty," he presumed—
  The " lead " he counted right—
The cause *one* bishop had assum'd
  With all *his* honest might.*

19.

And now *two others* led the way
  Fell treason to disown; †
That England's rightful king might sway
  And Richard's wrongs atone.

20.

Dear is a quiet home and life,
  Most dear its gentle joys;
Most hateful is the sword of strife,
  Which home and life destroys.‡

---

* *Thomas Mercks*, Bishop of Carlisle.—See Part II. and Note.
† The two Primates of Canterbury and York.—See Part VI.,
v. 10, and Note.
‡ Of " a quiet home and life," however, Lord Bardolph had no
longer any choice; for it will be seen in the extract of a letter from

21.

But dearer to the noble mind—
Dearer to honor's breast—
To right the wrong'd throughout mankind,
And against vice protest.*

22.

Better die young, than to grow old
In compromise with Evil,
And those who scruple not to " hold
A candle to the Devil ! " †

23.

Orders " *to hurry into Wales,*
Attendant on the king,
To crush Glendor," (whose cause he hails,)
Things to their climax bring.

24.

Revolt ? or *pander ?* which way choose ?
He cannot hesitate ;
He may not now the moments lose,
He must precipitate.

25.

Upon the daïs, in the state room,
Lord Bardolph took " Farewell ! "
First, of his brother, who is come
To hear all he would tell.

26.

Sir William Bardolph, brave and bluff,
Contrasted with the Baron ;
Though kind at heart, in manner rough,
The world was his " free warren."

27.

Both loyal, valiant, just, and true,
Yet each unlike his brother ;
The one in temper like the dew,
A sudden storm the other.

---

the council to the king—at the end of this Part VII.—that *he was
actually summoned to attend the king into Wales, there to suppress
the very cause which he was engaged to defend.*

* " Thou shalt, in any wise, rebuke thy neighbor, and not suffer
sin upon him."—Levit., xix., 17.——" Boldly rebuke vice, con-
stantly speak the truth, and patiently suffer for the truth's sake."
—Collect for John Baptist's Day.

† " Jesus said unto *Peter,* Get thee behind me, *Satan !* for thou
savorest not the things that be of God, but those that be of men.
Whosoever will save his life, shall lose it ; and whosoever will lose
his life for my sake, shall find it."—Matt., xvi., 21—26.

28.

The one, reflective and refin'd,
Discern'd varieties;
The other everything combin'd
Into two qualities.

29.

All hot or cold—all good or bad—
All difficult or plain;
All thrown aside, or captive made;
All pleasure, or all pain.

30.

Yet was Sir William good at need,
And though he hated sorrow,
Now he came with official speed
To know about the morrow.

31.

The Baron rose, with outstretch'd hand,
And anguish in his look,
About to give his last command,
And thus, confiding, spoke.

32.

"My brother dear, in my stead here
You will command the Fort,
And, if attack'd by Lancaster,
Secure—but fight it not.

33.

"Let no blood at our hearth be shed,
Let not the women weep;
If in great strength he should invade,
Hold parley from the Keep.

34.

"Bowmen and bargemen, pick and choose—
Knights—squires—men-at-arms—
Ever in readiness to use
At the first war's alarms.

35.

"Convey the Baroness and babes
To Pentney's holy cell;
Around them weave the surest webs
Of safety possible.*

---

* "Pentney, a prety Abbay, the ordinary buriall place, in ancient time, of the Noblemen and Gentlemen in this tract. Neere unto it lieth *Wormegay*, commonly *Wrongey*, which Reginald de Warren (brother of William de Warren, the second Earl of Surrey) had with his wife, of whom, as I have heard, he had the donation,

36.

"Their escort—ever on the watch,
Whether by day or night—
Thence to recover, and despatch
Them further out of sight.

37.

"Either *Lord Cromwell's* home, or thine,
A refuge will afford ;
And so, embrace me, brother mine,
And pledge thy solemn word."*

38.

Sir William answer'd zealously—
"While I have life and breath,
Thou shalt not find a fault in me,
Nor curse me after death.

39.

"Thy wife and children I will guard,
Thy territory too,
As I look up for heaven's award,
My brother, brave and true.

40.

"Who would not die to serve the man
Who only lives to show
All the good service that he can,
Either to high or low ?

41.

"Whose spirit soars (as I would mine !)
Up to you boundless God ;
Aiming among the stars to shine,
And shining on the road ? †

---

or *Maritagium* (as they used to speak in the law phrase) · and, by
his sonne's daughter, straitwayes it was transferred to the *Bardolphs*,
who, being Barons of great nobility, flourished a long time in
honorable estate, and bare, for their armes, *three cinque-foiles or*,
in *a shield azure*. The greatest part of whose inheritance, together
with the title, came to *Sir William Phelip*, and by his daughter
passed away to the Viscount Beaumont.—(See Camden's Britannia,
Northfolke, p. 481.)

   * The then Lord Cromwell was the brother of Lady (Avicia)
Bardolph ; and his home, Tatsall or Tattershall Castle, in Lincolnshire, was the home both of her own maiden and early married life.

   † "They that be wise shall shine as the brightness of the firma-
ment — as the stars for ever and ever."—Daniel, xii., 3.

42.

" Whose nobleness and tenderness
Would guard *me* like a shield,
And only wish to hear *me* bless
The comfort *he* can yield?

43.

" Who would not leave my *lifeless corse*
To menial services,
To Beings who have no remorse,
No pious decencies;

44.

" But hide it, as a sacred hoard,
And honor, as he would
The Body of our Blessed Lord,
The " Hero " Son of God! *

45.

" Brother! forgive my erring word,
If I have counsell'd wrong,
And thee from wisdom's way deterr'd,
To me the blame belong! †

46.

" By me this parting is ill borne,
Thine absence is a blight;
A sun gone down! a sea up torn!
A shipwreck at midnight!

47.

" Of thee, to all the world I boast,
But, with my brother gone,
" The world " to me is more than lost;
I hate it, and I scorn!"

48.

Each brother clasp'd his brother's hand,
Then fell upon his neck;
And, as in boyhood, unrestrain'd
Each press'd the other's cheek.

---

* " Unto us a Child is born—a Son is given; who shall be HEAD
over all things to the church, which is His Body; and these shall
be His TITLES—
    1. WONDERFUL COUNSELLOR!
    2. DIVINE HERO!
    3. FATHER OF THE LIFE TO COME!
    4. PEACE-MAKING PRINCE!"
—(*The Author's reading of* Isaiah, ix., 6.)
        † See Part VI., v. 85—86.

49.

Each understood his brother's soul—
 Ready to render life
To serve—to succour—to console
 In sorrow, or in strife.

*   *   *   *

50.

Sir William went. The Children came,
 The jewels of his heart ;
And thus he fram'd his words to *them*,
 To spare pain—using art.

51.

" Come hither, fondlings ! say, Farewell !
 And bid me lucky speed ;
And let your music-voices tell
 That you love me indeed.

52.

" Daisies, and roses of the spring !
 Pet buds of jessamine !
Dew drops serene and glittering !
 My rainbow ! my sunshine !

53.

" What can compare, my children fair,
 With all I think of you ?
With all I wish, of good and rare,
 To grace my daughters two ?

54.

" Sweet beings ! hush those hurtful sobs
 Shed not those precious tears !
I'll say no farewell word that robs
 Me of *hurrahs* and *cheers !*

55.

" Kisses I covet by the lot,
 And a warm heart embrace ;
But no wet drop my cheek to spot,
 And stain each pretty face.

56.

" Let me remember sunny smiles,
 Bright looks and merry eyes ;
Let me believe that Hope beguiles
 My Birds of Paradise !

57.

" Happy and gay, pass every day
  As free from fault as pain,
And to your *heavenly* Father pray
  Till *me* you see again.

58.

" He can shed honey-dew in store,
  He *creates* happiness ;
He can unite us all once more,
  And with each other bless.

59.

" 'T is He in whom we live and move,
  He keeps us in His sight ;
To Him we owe our mutual love,
  And every dear delight.

60.

" Ye darling pair ! my blessing share !
  And go tell her who waits
The word—that I must now repair
  Up to the hill-guard gates."

61.

The maidens went.   The Mother came,
  As from a dream awoke,
As one whose soul was out of frame,
  When thus the Baron spoke.

62.

" Belovéd woman ! beauteous wife !
  Heart's blood of my own heart ;
Best portion of our mingled life,
  God wills that we must part !

63.

" Not part in spirit ! oh ! not so !
  Not part in love divine !
Whate'er betide us, weal or woe,
  I'm thine, and thou art mine !

64.

Though absent, though engag'd in war,
  Though occupied with others,
The husband makes the wife *his* care,
  As the babe is the mother's.

65.

" And, as wean'd babes their mothers miss,
  Whom no one can replace,
So long I for the dearer bliss
  Of seeing thy dear face !

66.

" My soul shall hunger for thy soul,
My breath shall breathe of thee ;
The emotions which my deeds control
    Spring from thy charity.

67.

" The bread I eat, the wine I drink,
Whate'er I say, or do,
Is all more dainty when I think
    That we are one—not two !

68.

" My duties, both to man and God,
    Seem all more dignified ;
My very self I deem more good,
    By thy love sanctified.

69.

" Our children ! ah ! devote thy mind
    To them as part of me ;
Our daughters let me come and find
    Mirrors, Sweetheart, of thee !

70.

" Heaven, in its mercy, grant that aid
    We all and each require !
Blessings, like showers overhead,
    Only wait our desire.

71.

" Farewell ! Fruit blossom ! Treasure-trove !
    Aviee ! God made the *worm*,
And He will guard THEE while I rove
    His pleasure to perform.

72.

" In my barr'd breast, a mountain heaves,
    Eager to make escape,
When, like the moonlight through the leaves,
    Shines—through *my* mind—*thy* shape !

73.

" My moonlight, thou ! I the glad leaves !
    Till, when thou art withdrawn,
My soul no more life's joy perceives,
    'T is dark, as when unborn.

74.

" But, as the dead—the coffin bound—
    From death shall burst to life,
(At the Archangel's trumpet sound,
    With health and joy be rife !)

75.

"So (notwithstanding all around
    Be intermediate strife)
Shall I, with happy victory crown'd,
    Rush to my wife—my wife"—

76.

With tender strength her form he clasp'd,
    She as an ivy clung ;
While mouth to mouth they glued, then gasp'd,
    Arm-bonded, but heart-wrung.

77.

Each turn'd aside the head to hide
    The truant tear that sprung ;
(Lest the one should the other chide)
    And like two lilies hung.

78.

But true love may not be conceal'd,
    Dissembled, or reproach'd ;
He longs to have his truth reveal'd,
    When his dear life is touch'd.

79.

No foolish pride—no faulty shame—
    No secret self-reserve—
No affectation haunted them—
    Only—paramount love.*

80.

"O my soul's lord!" the lady said,
    "Live only to return,
Here to repose thy precious head,
    Then I may cease to mourn.

81.

"Sweetheart !" quotha ? what boots the heart
    That beats in woman's breast ?
Who can appreciate her smart ?
    What hope has she of rest ?

82.

"Distress and dread! without the power
    To hinder or escape ;
The very joys we have in store
    Turn into sorrow's shape.

83.

"O for some lonely ocean isle,
    From kings and quarrels far,
Where only works of peace beguile,
    Without the sound of war !

* "Let love be without dissimulation."—Romans, xii., 9.

84.

" Mysterious is our destiny,
    Our life is all un-rest ;
Though love itself is heavenly,
    Heaven does not make it blest.

85.

" Hereafter, Bardolph ! may we meet
    (God speed the weary time !)
In some obscure but safe retreat,
    From sorrow and from crime ! "

86.

Then anguish burst its prison bars,
    The floodgates of her eyes ;
And for a while—[those brimming stars
    Eclips'd]—she spoke in sighs.

87.

Then overcame that weak indulge,
    But pray'd him still to stop ;
His plans, his projects to divulge,
    And feed her heart with hope.

88.

Patient and willing he complied—
    All that he could he said ;
And then they linger'd, side by side,
    Arm-linkt, hand-lockt, lip-wed.

89.

Into each other's soul's abyss
    They gaz'd—with quivering face—
Then met one last impassion'd kiss,
    Then clos'd one last embrace—

90.

Repeated—because each last one
    Refus'd to be the *last ;*
Though she said, in an undertone,
    " Death's bitterness is past ! "

91.

The husband wrestled with the chief,
    And all his might subdued ;
Till crushing thoughts that sought relief,
    He, like a statue, stood.

92.

Speechless, he held his hands aloft,
    Then over her he bent—
As blessing earnestly and oft,
    And thus receding—went !

    *   *   *   *

93.

He went—she watch'd! then roam'd about,
 All haggard at the heart—
Too full of grief; and then she sought
 Her sorrow to impart.

94.

" To whom ? and whither can I go ?
 An early widow doom'd;
Who cares—who can abide the woe
 I carry to the tomb ? "

95.

She rais'd her head—she view'd the sky—
 She peer'd into the vault—
As if to search out the Most High
 And blame Him for the fault !

96.

At the same moment—horrorstruck
 With her impiety—
" O Christ ! if my heart must be broke—
 Leave me not utterly ! "

97.

Down on her knees, in her own bower,
 Beside the bed of state,
She sank to seek a Saviour's power,
 Where Bardolph lay of late.

98.

As though the bed contain'd one dead,
 And him a bloody corse,
With funeral trappings overlaid,
 And certain was her loss ;—

99.

" O Mercy's God ! give me thy grace,
 Without which I despair;
Open mine eyes to see Thy Face,
 Thou that art everywhere !

100.

" Disdain not thy poor creature's cry—
 This being is thine own ;
If I am hated, let me die,
 Or hear my piteous moan ! "

101.

She said, and stay'd—in silence stay'd,
 And listen'd for a thought ;
And as her spirit upward stray'd,
 This answer back it brought.

19

102.

"Peace I leave with thee—Peace I give—
My Peace is my bequest ;
Because I live, my friends shall live,
In ME have Peace and Rest.

103.

"In ME have always Hope and Faith,
In ME have constant Trust ;
Be firm and faithful unto death,
I'll raise thee from the dust.

104.

"More than is taken, thou shalt have,
More joy than thou *hast* known ;
HE who could overcome the grave
Can give thee back THINE OWN.

105.

"Turn to thy duties of the day,
Thy task of every hour ;
Pray, pray, and work ; work, work, and pray,
As God doth give thee power!" *

106.

She sought her girls ; she sought the priest,
The chaplain of the home ;
She had *the Holy Altar* dress'd,
Which the Pope sent from Rome.†

---

* "By two immutable things, in which it is impossible for God to *lie*, we have a strong consolation, who have fled for refuge to the hope set before us, as an anchor of the soul, sure and stedfast, even JESUS !"—Hebrews, vi., 18—20.

† Although the Pope really resided at *Avignon* at the time of this transaction, nevertheless the Pope's presence any where would be the head quarters of the *Church of Rome ;* and therefore *Rome* and not *Avignon* is recorded in the text. John Lord Bardolph, the grandfather of the subject of this memoir, had married Elizabeth, only child of Roger Lord Damory and Elizabeth eldest daughter of Gilbert de Clare, Earl of Gloster, and Joan of Acra, daughter of King Edward I. and Queen Eleanor ; and was, it appears, sent on a mission by the King into Italy, to negotiate the return of Pope Urban V. to Rome, who then (1363) was residing at *Avignon,* as several Popes had done before him, since the year 1304 ; and there, in Italy, Lord Bardolph died, Saturday, 31st July, 1363. But, on a previous similar occasion, when visiting the court of Pope Clement VI., in 1352, that prelate evinced his high esteem of John Lord Bardolph by the donation and permission of a *moveable altar,* in those days a very great favor indeed ; and the grant, or *bull,* conferring this *altar,* is thus, in Latin, worded :—" Clemens episcopus, servus servorum Dei, dilecto filio, nobili viro, Johanni Bardolf, militi, et dilecte in Christo filio, nobili mulieri, Elizabethe, ejus uxori, Norwicensis diocesis, salutem et apostolicam benedictionem. Sincere devotionis affectus, qui

107.

While the priest pray'd, her hand she laid
On each child by her side ;
Intreating God's grace to be shed,
Whatever might betide.

108.

And every day in this same way,
And at the hour of noon,
Humbly did they together pray
For *him* the *absent one.*

109.

And surely in High *Heaven's* abode
Some sympathy was felt
For wife and children seeking God
And sighing as they knelt?

110.

And surely upon earth *they* shar'd
That calm and quietude
Which, if with godless woe compar'd,
Is a beatitude?

111.

And surely not in vain for *him*
Did wife and children vow,
Who, when the light of life grew dim
And death bedew'd his brow—

112.

Still a strange *triumph* could enjoy,
Still a fair *sight* could see,
Of Angel Guards round him deploy,
All singing—VICTORY!

ad nos et Romanam geritis ecclesiam, non indigne meruit ut petitionibus vestris, &c., quas ex devotionis fervore prodire conspicimus, quantum cam domino possumus, favorabiliter annuamus.
Hinc est quod nos, vestris devotis supplicationibus inclinati, ut
liceat vobis habere *altare portabile* cum reverentia et honore, super
quod, in locis ad hoc convenientibus et honestis possit quilibet
vestrorum per proprium sacerdotem ydoneum, missam et alia divina
officia, sine juris alieni prejudicio, in vestra presencia facere celebrari, devotioni vestre tenore presencium indulgemus. Nulli verò
omnino hominum liceat hanc paginam nostre concessionis infringere,
vel ejus ausu temerario cohibere. Si quis autem hoc attemptare
presumpserit, indignacionem omnipotentis Dei et beatorum Petri et
Pauli Apostolorum ejus se noverit incursurum. Datum Avinione
VII. idus Augusti Pontificatus nostri anno undecimo," (7 August,
1352).—(Lib. de Antiquis Legibus, p. 118, pref.)

The following passage in a letter from the council
addressed to the king, in which they acknowledge the
receipt of the king's letters, dated Worcester, 8th
day of May, 1405, contains the earliest notice of
Lord Bardolf's movements on this occasion :—

"—— d'autre part, notre tres redoute et sovercin
seigneur, plese vous savoir que à la reception de les
susdites vos lettres, nous n'avions receu novelles
autres que nous n'escrivismes devers vous pardevant:
mais, tot aprez reportez nous etoit tant par aucuns
du conseil de Monseigneur Johan, votre filz, come
par autres dignes de foy, coment le Sire de Bardolf
se transporta privement ja tarde vers les parties du
Northe, ses manoirs et places tout desolées, et les
biens et chateux d'iceux emportez, dount nous nous
merveillons grandement, puis-que, come nous pensons, il avoit en commandement de part de vous de
soy transporter en present en votre compagnie es
parties de Gales pur ceste foiz"

Thereupon, the king moved towards the North,
and when at Derby, wrote on the 28th day of May
following, to his council, in these terms :—

" Reverents peres en Dieu et tres chiers et foiaulx.
Nous vous salvons souvent, et pensons bien qu' il est
venuz ja tarde a votre notice comment le conte de
Northumberland, le conte Marischal, et le Sire de
Bardolf, et autres de leurs adherentz es parties del
Northe, se sont levez encontre nostre mageste roiale,
et coment le dit conte Mareschal tient la champe
ovec toute le povoir qu' il a, et puet lever de notre
peuple en le pays sur son chemyn, plusieurs maugre
leur."

The first assembly of the forces of the insurgents
took place at Topcliff, Northallerton, and Cleaveland,
under these leaders—

> Sir John Fauconberg,
> Sir Ralph Hastings,
> Sir John Fitz Randolf,
> And Sir John Colvyle of the Dale,

} chivalers
who,

prior to the date of this letter, had been routed, and
put to flight, and made prisoners by the royal forces,
under Prince John of Lancaster, the Earl of Westmoreland, the Lord Fitzhugh and others.

The next assembly is that alluded to in the king's
letter, under the Archbishop of York, the Earl Marshal and of Nottingham, Sir William Plumpton, Sir
Robert Lamplugh, and Sir Robert Persay, chivalers,
at Shipton on the Moor, a hamlet in the parish of

NOTE TO PART VII.

Overton, within the forest of Galtres, where, on the 29th day of May, *these several leaders were made prisoners through treachery.*

Upon the receipt of intelligence of this disaster, the Earl of Northumberland and Lord Bardolf retreated into Scotland; and before the second day of July, the castles of Prudhoe and Warkworth had been yielded up to the king. For this *misconduct* (?), in the Parliament begun at Westminister 1st March, 1406 (7 Henry IV.), and finished at the same place 22nd December (8 Henry IV.), Thomas Lord Bardolf, after divers summons to appear before the king, was, on Saturday, the 5th December, 1407, declared to be convicted of treason, as being leagued with Henry Earl of Northumberland, and Robert III. (lately)* King of Scotland, and with the rebels in Wales, and that, for these and other treasons, with the Scots and Welsh, against the person of the lord the king; the said Henry de Percy and Thomas de Bardolf be convicted as traitors to the said lord the king, and that, in case they could be taken, should be drawn, hung, and beheaded at the pleasure of the said lord the king; and that the said lord the king should have the forfeiture "de tous les chastells, seigneuries, manoirs, terres, tenements, rentz, services, fees, et avoesons et quelconques autres possessions es queux les dits Henry de Percy et Thomas de Bardolf, le sisme jour de May, ou depuis."—(See Lib. de Ant. Leg., p. 143, pref.)

* Robert III., King of Scotland, died on Palm Sunday, 4th April, 1406.

WERMIGEY.

PART VIII.

WHITSUNTIDE DESECRATIONS;

OR

POLITICAL EXPEDIENCY ON SHIPTON MOOR.

A.D. 1405.

> " I saw, under sun, the Place of Judgement—
> That wickedness was there !
> And the Place of Righteousness—
> That iniquity was there !
> And I said in my heart
> God shall judge the Righteous and the Wicked."
>
> ECCLESIASTES, III., 16—17.

" For the children of this world are, in their generation, wiser than the children of Light."—LUKE, XVI., 8.

" It was said of Tiberius Cæsar, in a satirical libel—

> ———————" regnabit sanguine multo
> Ad regnum quisquis venit ab exilio."

that is

> " Who, first exil'd, if after crown'd,
> His reign with blood shall much abound."
>
> *Suetonius*, lib. iii., cap. 59.

" This the king (Henry IV.) verified in his person, who, coming out of banishment, could not support his title and estate, but by shedding much blood of subjects. For, not content with the lives of *Thomas Mowbray* the Earl Marshall, and the Archbishop *Scrope*, he pursueth the *Earl of Northumberland* and the *Lord Bardolph*, with an invincible army of seven and thirty thousand men."— *History of England*, by *John Speed.*

The March of the Wermigey Men off the Hill Guard
(or West-Brig Ward) Parade Ground, A.D. 1405.

1.

From Norfolk to Northumberland
  We'll gaily sally forth,
If those, at home, will forward stand
  And hail our journey north.

2.

From Norfolk to Northumberland
  We'll wend our weary way,
Fearless of any hostile band
  If those, at home, will pray.

3.

From Norfolk to Northumberland
  We'll go to fight and bleed,
Rejoicing in our Chief's command
  And trusting in God's speed.

4.

From Norfolk to Northumberland
  To conquer, or to die;
To right our king, with heart and hand
  We'll march, and sing "Good bye!"

5.

The Music cheer'd the marching host
  So long as it might last ;
And so lasted till was lost
  The home from which they past.

6.

But, when it stay'd and no cheer made
  To help the heavy tramp,
The spirits fade, and the night shade
  Fell like a wintry damp.

7.

Then came the moral force in play,
  The powers of the mind,
To stem re-action, and to sway
  The sadness left behind.

8.

In the fresh morn with strength new born,
  Conversible are men ;
But road-wore, foot-sore, heart-forlorn,
  They march in silence then.

9.

In silence think, each his own thought,
    As wearily they plod,
Reviewing life-time and the lot
    Dispens'd to them by God.

10.

Poor fellows! O that soldiers all
    Had nothing to regret,
Except hard fortune, and the " call "
    Which causes some to fret.

11.

O that, while wearing war's attire,
    They were Christ's volunteers ;
That they would carry *sword* and *fire*
    To Satan his frontiers ! *

12.

O that, while *patriotic slaves*,
    They would from vice be free ;
Fight their souls' foes, like him who braves
    A shotted battery !

13.

Who would not be a soldier then—
    Who would the glory miss ?
Who would not be a veteran
    In such a force as this ?

14.

Lord Bardolph was a " *Flugle* "-man—
    He studied so to be ;
And, what one does, another can
    In Christian chivalry.

15.

The race which all are call'd to run
    Would be, indeed, unfair
If made impossible to one
    Call'd to be Christ's joint-heir.

16.

And God, we know, is not unjust,
    The Good Lord died for all,
Excepting those who WILL be curst
    And are *im*-placable.

---

* In the Christian panoply, the *Sword* of the Spirit, which is the Word, or Truth, of God, is not only a *sharp* sword, and a *piercing* sword, and *double-edged*, but it is also a *flaming* sword, burning (as well as cutting every way) through every thing, to guard the Tree of Life, and *foil* the *fiery* weapons of the wicked.—See Ephesians. vi., 16—17 ; Hebrews, iv., 12 ; Genesis, iii., 21.

17.
There is *no* wrath in the Most High,
No hatred tow'rds mankind ;
In man it is tow'rds Him we spy
Hatred and wrath combin'd ! *

18.
Perversion—falsehood—lack of faith,
(Things we profess to scorn)
These are what work our final death,
And make this world forlorn.

19.
The march continued, day by day,
Until at *Shipton Moor*
They join'd the forces of *Moubray*,
And also *Percy's* power—

20.
Archbishop *Scroope*, Lord *Falconbridge*,
Lord *Hastings* too, and then
Muster'd, upon an average,
Some twenty thousand men.

21.
Then might have been a battle fought,
A glorious victory gain'd,
Had the *right man* the *right place* got
And for that been retain'd.

22.
But compliment to character,
For *dignity* or *age*,
Instead of leadership for war,
Blotted another page.

23.
The king's lieutenant, *Westmoreland*,
Had not an equal force,
But greater skill at his command
For bettering the worse.

24.
Us'd *artifice* and *policy*—
Pretended a *good-will* ;
Play'd on the Priest's *credulity*,
And made him " pay the bill ! "

---

* "God is Love!" (1 John, iv., 7—8) " whose *property* is *always* to have *mercy*."—Book of Common Prayer; the Prayer before that for the High Court of Parliament.

25.

The good Archbishop he *cajol'd*
To let his troops take rest,
Then took him prisoner, and told
Him he had been in *jest !* *

26.

Gaily the *Arch*-Lieutenant grinn'd,
And chuckled at his feat ;
Nay, laugh'd aloud, that he had pinn'd
The Churchman so complete.

27.

" Success ! all glory to success ! "
Said *Lancaster* when told ;
" *Westmoreland* with his cleverness
Is worth his weight in gold ! "

---

* Sir Richard Baker's account is this :—" *Henry Piercy*, Earl
of Northumberland, *Richard Scroop*, Archbishop of York, *Thomas
Mowbray*, Earl Marshall, the Lords *Hastings*, *Falconbridge*, and
Bardolf, with divers others, conspired at a time appointed, to meet
upon *Yorkswold Downs*, and there bid defiance to King Henry.
Articles of Grievance were framed, and set up in all public places,
which drew multitudes to be partakers of the enterprize. But now
Ralph Nevil, Earl of Westmoreland, with the Lord *John*, the
king's third son, the Lord *Henry Fitzhughes*, *Ralph Evers*, and
Robert Humphreville, made head against them ; and coming into
a plain in the forest of Galtree, they sat down right against the
Archbishop and his forces, which were twenty thousand. But
Westmoreland perceiving the enemy's forces to be far more than
theirs, he used this policy He sent to the Archbishop, demanding
why he would raise forces against the king ? who answering that
his arms were not against the king, but in his own defence, whom
the king, at the instigation of sycophants, had threatened, withal
sent him a scroll of their grievance, which Westmoreland read, and
seemed to approve, and thereupon desired a conference with him.
The Archbishop, more credulous than wise, persuaded the Earl
Marshal to go with him to the place, appointed to confer. The
Articles were read, and allowed of, and thereupon *Westmoreland*
seeming to commiserate the soldiers, having been in armor all day,
and weary, wished the Archbishop to acquaint his party, as he
would his, with their mutual agreement ; and so shaking hands,
in most courtly friendship, drank with him. Whereupon the
soldiers were willed to disband, and repair home, which they had
no sooner done, when a troop of horse, which, in a colorable manner, had made a show to depart, wheeled about, and returned, and
being come in sight of the Earl of *Westmoreland*, arrested both the
Archbishop and the *Earl Marshal*, and brought them both prisoners
to the king at Pomfret ; who passing from thence to York, the
prisoners likewise were carried thither, and beheaded."

28.

There is a maxim amongst men,
" *That every wile is fair,*
The object they desire to gain,
In Wedlock, Wealth, or War ! "

29.

Many such maxims are in vogue
To make wrong *right* appear,
Because convenient to the rogue
Who stops at nothing here.

30.

But of such there is never need
With those who take delight
In weeding crime-craft from their creed
And making Honor bright.

31.

What *mean* the Laws of Chivalry ?
What *do* the Brave admire ?
How *can* the Foe-Worlds so agree,
The lower and the higher ?

32.

Scroop, Moubray, Falconbridge, Hastings,
All fell into the snare ;
Entrapp'd by a rogue's reasonings,
All four beheaded were.

33.

Percy and *Bardolph* made escape,
Seeing the treachery ;
While Satan's *ape*, in his own shape,
Perform'd this butchery.

34.

They fled amain to Scotland then,
And *Henry* in their wake,
With *thirty-seven thousand* men,
Could not them overtake.

35.

Great was his eagerness and haste,
On deeds of vengeance bent,
And anger terribly express'd
At the disappointment.

36.

His teeth he gnash'd—his fury lash'd—
Like a wild lion's tail—
His arms he clash'd—his sword he dash'd
On many a coat of mail.

37.

"By God's soul!" swore that Monarch grim,
  "On any future field,
Percy and Bardolph, limb by limb,
  Like vermin shall be kill'd.

38.

"Meanwhile, their *castles* shall be raz'd,
  Their *lands* confiscate be,
Their *heads* by auction be apprais'd,
  Or so be done to me!"

39.

Nathless, they fled, and well they sped
  From avarice and hate;
As not yet dead, with blood unshed,
  Still they might hinder Fate.

40.

Ambitious, each pursuing man
  Endeavour'd to come near;
But woe betided *Henry's* van
  When they reach'd *Percy's* rear.

41.

The arrow flight, the sabre bright,
  Made a sore havoc then;
Disorder—death—and pale affright
  Perplex'd the hunting men.

42.

Percy and Bardolph made retreat
  A frequent victory,
For, as their state was desperate,
  So was their energy.

43.

At times, they slew the daring scouts
  Who track'd their weary way;
At times, broke bridges, block'd up routes,
  To stop the enemy.

44.

Over the Border—out of reach,
  They sought a noble Scot,
Lord *Fleming*, who, in northern speech,
  Kindly bade them "Fear not!" *

"On the East side of *Sterlinghire* in Scotland, at *Cumbernauld*
(near Callendar Castle belonging to the Barons of Levin, some)
dwells the family of the *Barons Fleming*, bestowed on them by
King Robert Bruce, for their good service in valiantly and loyally

45.

" Your tyrant foe, loud let him low ;
    By all that 's leal and true,
As you did harbor *Douglas*, so
    Will *Fleming* harbor you.

46.

" Surely, you king must come to die
    In God's good time at least ;
The Deil, no doubt, has liberty
    On human flesh to feast—

47.

" But for awhile ; this cannibal,
    When glutted with the gore,
Will one day make a woesome wail
    That he can gorge no more.

48.

" Surely, that day is over nigh
    The nearer for his haste ;
'T is for our sins we have to sigh,
    When thus we are laid waste.

49.

" Take comfort, friends—God has His ends,
    In all our sufferings ;
These demons back to hell He sends,
    His saints to glory brings."

50.

Lord Bardolph hugg'd the genial Scot,
    Return'd his honest gripe,
For seeking thus to soothe their lot,
    And Percy's tears to wipe.

51.

Northumberland ! his day was o'er,
    His splendid prospects gone ;
Oft would he murmur out—"Hotspur !
    My son—my son—my son !

52.

" Thou that wast to have been the brother
    Of England's rightful king !
Now dead—dead—dead—both one and other—
    And I an outcast thing ! "

---

defending their country, upon which account they also had con-
ferred on them the honor of hereditary *High Chamberlain of Scotland*; and, subsequently by King James the VI., the title of *Earls
of Wigtown*." (See Camden, Scotland, Stirlingshire, p. 921.)

53.
A broken heart—a blighted hope—
  A dismal conscience cloud—
Ill serve to keep the courage up—
  In spirit he was bow'd.

54.
Yet Bardolph cheer'd his stricken friend,
  And gave to life a zest ;
" The darkest day," he said, " must end—
  In heaven there is rest.

55.
"Though Love, and Peace, and Wealth, and Power
  A short time we enjoy,
In that short time what evils more
  May with them breed annoy.

56.
" Our pleasures may promote our doom,
  Our sorrows work our good ;
Even at home there *may* be gloom,
  And *must* be, without God !

57.
" Live we like men who do *not die*,
  But only *change estate ;*
The soldiers of the King Most High
  Should ever be elate.*

58.
" While we have warlike work to do,
  We need a warlike heart ;
Our days are few—death is our due—
  Yet must we act our part."

59.
For still a part had they to act,
  More tragic than all past ;
Three years of exile to enact,
  With bloody end at last.

60.
Their noble host was not allow'd
  To entertain them long ;
The malice of the *mean* and *proud*
  Together was too strong.

---

* "Jesus said, He that believeth in ME, shall NEVER DIE :"—
John, xi., 25—26.

61.

According to King David's words—
" *The wicked cannot sleep*
Without the comfort crime affords "—*
Though it make angels weep.

62.

" Crime," which they hunger for and thirst
As for their proper food,
Which they devour—till disgust
Makes vomit up in blood.†

63.

" Crime," which they covet as a treasure
(Although the cost be death !)
In which they revel and take place
As in their life and breath.

64.

It is a Moral mystery
Which Science cannot solve,
" As soon as they are born they *lie*,
And *vice* is their resolve."‡

65.

That upon which the spirit feeds,
That which men hate and scorn,
(Whatever be their title deeds)
That proves who are *base-born*.

66.

" Base-born " was Lancaster of Gaunt,
" Base-born " that Scottish crew,
Who for the base bribes they would want
Base work for him would do.

67.

With him, some countrymen of *Fleming*,
For such *base* bribes agreed,
Without appearing or beseeming,
To do the *basest* deed.

68.

Take his two guests, dead or alive,
By a *base* stratagem ;
And, if they could not that contrive,
Then *basely* murder *him !*

---

* Psalm xxxvi., 4 ; and Proverbs, iv., 16.
† Like *Judas*, who, after betraying the innocent blood for a
little money, *brought again* the reward of his iniquity, *flung down*
the silver pieces, and then went and *hanged himself*, and falling
headlong, burst asunder, and all his bowels gushed out."—See
Matthew, xxvii., 3—6 : and Acts, i., 18—19.
‡ Psalm lviii., 3.

69.

The good Lord *Fleming* guess'd the plot—
That plot to them betray'd ;
And, when they from the danger got,
Was murder'd in their stead ! *

70.

Bravo! great Lancaster of Gaunt!
Hero of Bolingbroke ;
The British Lion thou didst mount
Did, with thy praises, choke.

71.

Proudly he caper'd up and down
[*Like that great roaring one†*
Who also covets Heaven's crown
And envies Heaven's throne !]

72.

That great obstreperous old fool,
So easily cajol'd,
Through *fear*, to let the *crafty* rule,
Through *avarice*, be sold.

73.

The British Lion—sad to tell—
Bray'd like a British Ass!
He gloried in a Fiend of Hell,
And made himself as *base*.

74.

Simply because that Fiend could ride
And cow the quaking beast,
And, with him, blood and bones divide,
And relish such a feast.

75.

Historians praise the uppermost
Who live in their own day,
Not caring how the *truth* it cost,
So long as *cash* it pay.

---

* The historian *Speed* thus notices this event:— "The king
being again in want of money, after long unwillingness and delay,
the Parliament furnished him, rather overcome with weariness in
contradiction, than for any great good will. Some of his treasure
was employed, as it seems, upon *secret practices* with the *Scots*,
that the Earl of *Northumberland* and the Lord *Bardolfe* might be
delivered into his hands, in exchange for some *Scots*. Whereupon
they fled into *Wales*, and the *Scots*, missing their purpose, slew
David Lord *Fleming* for discovering their intention to his distressed
guests, (as, by the laws of honor and hospitality, he was obliged)—
which filled *Scotland* with civil discords."

† 1 Peter, v., 8 ; and Luke, x., 18 ; and Rev., xii., 7—10.

76.

Even great Shakespeare could revile
And ridicule these lords,
To make Lancastrian Tudor smile,
When none could check his words.

77.

That mighty mind could stoop so low
And mockingly parade
Misfortune—in *the good cause*, too,
Better left in the shade.*

78.

Away to Wales and to Glendôr
The persecuted men
Fled to escape the searching power
Of the usurper then.

79.

But not in Wales could they abide
When Glendôr was hard press'd ;
Prince Harry his young talons tried
To rifle that bird's nest.

80.

Harry of Monmouth—" Prince of Wales "—
Most eager was to fit on
That new style, and turn the scales
Against the " ancient Briton."

81.

Therefore they fled away to France—
To Flanders—and again
To Scotland, where another chance
Offer'd the battle plain.†

---

* One of the old historians (B., C., D. or S.), worshipping the
" golden calf of Lancaster," and alluding to the unrest and pater-
nal grief of Earl Percy for the loss of Hotspur, *barbarously* writes
that " *the death of his son stuck in his stomach !*" And, according to Shakespeare, the glorious Hotspur was killed, *not* " riding
at the head of battel," *but* in a fight on foot (!)—*not* " by some unknown hand," but by the very son of the usurper (!)—a boy of
17 (!!)—on his first appearance in the field (!!!) According to
Shakespeare, also, Thomas Lord Bardolph was a premature (*i.e.*,
cowardly) *run-away* from Shrewsbury to Earl Percy, with *false
news* of victory! and his name is ascribed to, and confounded with,
one of the low companions in debauchery of the same riotous son
of the usurper!

† Sir Richard Baker thus records this historic item :—"*North-
umberland* and *Bardolfe*, after they had been in *Wales*, *France* and
Flanders, to raise a power against King *Henry*, returned back into
Scotland; and, after a year, with a great power of *Scots*, entered
England, and came into *Yorkshire*, making great spoil and waste
as they passed ; but Sir Thomas Rokesby, Sheriff of *York*, levying

82.

In the meantime, *at home* befel
  Another mis-adventure—
Despatches seiz'd, and a *false tale*
  Sent on—them to encounter.

83.

Lord Bardolf had a serving man
  Who, in those days forlorn,
Him *friended*, as some nobly can,
  Although in serfdom born.

84.

John Thurstan lov'd his feudal lord,
  When each was yet a boy ;
His heart's devotion he outpour'd
  Before he yet knew why.

85.

He was not dazzl'd by his state,
  He did not fear his power ;
He was not anxious to be great
  Beneath the Badge he wore.

86.

He stirr'd not others' jealousy
  By undeserv'd promotion ;
Of what he wish'd, or car'd, to be,
  Not many had a notion.

87.

He simply lov'd *because he lov'd*,
  And that there was a charm,
A centre joy, round which he mov'd,
  A sun, that made him warm.

88.

An object worthy of esteem,
  A being to admire ;
Who, high as he must always seem,
  Still hinted something higher.

89.

Thurstan would often volunteer
  Responsibility ;
Always to be the Baron near,
  Became his orderly.

the forces of the county upon *Bramham Moor*, gave them battle, in
which *Northumberland* was slain, *Bardolfe* taken, but wounded to
death, and the rest put to flight."—To which the historian *Speed*
adds that " the Abbot of *Hales*, because he was taken fighting on
the Earl's behalf, had sentence to die, which was executed by
hanging."

90.

Ready to show a daring zeal
When others fell behind,
As if to make his master feel
The stature of his mind.

91.

Ambitious to make proof that he
Could be a benefactor ;
And though a man of low degree,
Might he his chief's protector—

92.

Might be still greater than the great,
Still richer than the rich ;
Might make them bankrupt in his debt,
By deeds no pay could reach—

93.

The humblest works he undertook,
The hardest he would scan ;
Soldier, or sicknurse, groom, or cook,
Thurstan was the best man.

94.

For speed in peril, for success
In duties to be done,
Those, who might envy, would confess
None equall'd trusty " John."

95.

It was a pleasure exquisite
To know he was expected ;
And that he could confer delight
By services effected.

96.

The Messengers of Heaven thus
Indulge a Holy Pride,
When they convey some good to us,
Or turn some ill aside.

97.

'Tis then they plume their silvery wings,
Which joy thrills—like a breeze,
When, on a summer eve, it springs
Up in the aspen trees.*

---

* There is a fine specimen of the white-leafed aspen now florish-
ing in a lane (off the Lynn and Bury road) leading to the Wermigey Priory Ground, which suggested this comparison; and it is a
pleasure at any time in summer to watch and wonder at its ever-
varying and mysterious movements.

98.

So *Thurstan* grew a godlike soul,
For he learn'd from the Saviour
That dignity means self-control
And wealth, a kind behaviour.

99.

That happiness is what we give
Reflected in the mind ;
That which we sow, is sure to leave
A harvesting behind.

100.

During the flight from Shipton Moor,
John was the Baron's shadow ;
To gain that house, he was the door,
The window, and the ladder.

101.

To guard that fort, he was the moat,
No passage but by him ;
And death soon rattl'd in his throat
Who tried to ford that stream.

102.

When they reach'd Scotland safe and well,
John took the Baron's letters,
In Wermigey the news to tell,
And comfort the home fretters.

103.

Again, he carried into Wales
The cheer his lord requir'd ;
As the ship sails through stormy gales,
So peril him inspir'd.

104.

John Thurstan was the harbinger
And cherisher of hope ;
When any one gave way to fear,
His spirit was a prop.

105.

Both mind and body had a fund
Of enterprize and glee ;
Just as a ball on the rebound,
So trouble flouted he.

106.

And yet he was a serious man
And full of solemn thought ;
His cheerfulness was partly plan,
Religion's true result.

107.

A noble fellow—though untaught—
As there have many been,
To show that God is never sought
By honest hearts in vain.

108.

In July, fourteen-hundred-seven,
He carried a despatch
Again to Scotland, where now even
His lord was on the watch.

109.

So likewise were his lurking foes,
Who intercepted *John ;*
And, after interchanging blows,
Arrested him thereon.

110.

Rifled and ransack'd of his trust,
In a dark den secur'd,
Fetter'd and manacled, *to rust,*
During six months immur'd.

111.

Yet was not his brave soul depriv'd
Of all his consolation ;
While he lay bound, his lord surviv'd ;
Release !—was desolation !

112.

Percy and Bardolph while at large
Harass'd the king with fear;
Not till their deaths would he discharge
This faithful follower.*

---

* In the preface to the *Liber de Antiquis Legibus* (page 145) it
is recorded that "in the year 1407, a servant of Lord Bardolf,
named *John,* was taken with letters, and arrested, and committed
to the charge of the Lord de Grey," (Reynold Lord Grey de Ruthin,)
"in whose custody he remained from the 6th day of July up to the
20th day of February, 230 days," [that is, *until the day after the
battle of Bramham Moor,* and *the deaths of Lord Bardolf and Earl
Percy ;* for—] "in this interval of time, early in the year 1408, the
Earl and Lord Bardolf, *deceived by false intelligence,* entered Northumberland, and having been joined by several adherents of the
Earl, advanced into Yorkshire. At Thirsk, they published a
manifesto, containing their reason for being in arms, and at Knaresborough were joined by Sir Nicholas Tempest, whence they continued their route through Wetherby, over Bramham Moor, in the
direction of Haslewood, where they were encountered by the forces
under the command of Sir Thomas Rokeby, Sheriff of Yorkshire,
whom they supposed to be friendly to their cause."

WERMIGEY.

PART IX.

CIVIL WAR—THE BATTLE OF BRAMHAM MOOR.

Sunday, 19th February, 1408.

I. *The Sycophant's Information.*

"*Harcourt.* From enemies, Heaven keep your Majesty!
And, when they stand against you, may they fall
As those that I am come to tell you of!
The Earl Northumberland and the Lord Bardolph,
With a great power of English, and of Scots,
Are, by the Sheriff of Yorkshire, overthrown."

SHAKESPEARE, *Henry IV.*, Part 2, Act 4, Sc. 4.

II. *The Sufferer's Consolation.*

"Rejoice not against me, O mine enemy—
When I fall—I shall arise again!"

MICAH, vii., 8.

III. *The Saviour's Injunction.*

"Fear not them which kill the body."

MATT., x., 28.

"Speak unto the children of Israel—That they go FORWARD!"

EXOD., xiv., 15.

"Tu, ne cede malis; sed contrà, audentior ito!"

VIRGIL, *Æneid*, vi., 95.

(Author's free translation.)

Flinch not from Fate: front it, and forward go.
A triple triumph tracks terrestrial woe!
The *World*—the *Wicked*—thine own *Frailty* know.
They do but break thy shell at every blow,
To help thee *wing up* whither I AM now!

1.

God trains His Soldiers as He train'd
His Son—their Captain—Christ! *
Heaven's Glory is not to be gain'd
But by Earth sacrific'd!

2.

Duties, though hard, they must fulfil—
  Orders, they must obey—
Endure the discipline and drill—
  Or Soldiers none are they.†

3.

Nature may shrink—and shrink it must—
  And shrink it ever did ;
Since Sin it *wedded*—it is just,
  Till, of Sin, it be rid.

4.

And only Death dissolves the tie
  To which it was ensnar'd
By its disobedient folly !
  So Sin's fate *must* be shar'd.

5.

Till Death—till Death—till parted breath
  Has seal'd the soul's *divorce*—‡
Sought, first, by penitence and faith,
  And shouldering the Cross ! §

6.

Percy and *Bardolph* thus were train'd ;
  And though despoil'd of all,
What matter'd it, if Heaven they gain'd,
  And answer'd Heaven's call ?

7.

Weary of exile—sick for home—
  Absent almost three years ;
In vain displaying while they roam
  Their many hopes and fears ;

8.

At length, in Scotland, they retrieve
  The time and labor lost ;
A bandit army they contrive
  And raise a mighty host.

---

* "He made the Captain of their Salvation perfect through sufferings."—Hebrews, ii., 10.

† "Thou, therefore, endure hardship, as a good soldier of Jesus Christ."—" And please Him, who hath chosen thee to be a soldier."—1 Tim., ii., 3—4.

‡ "O wretched man that I am ! who shall deliver me from this body of death ? I thank God—through Jesus Christ our Lord."—Romans, vii., 24.

§ "Jesus said--If any man will come after Me, let him deny himself, and *take up his cross*, and follow Me."—Matt., xvi., 24.

9.

The Border clans their nobles all
In cluster'd numbers bring,
England to help to disenthral
Of England's *robber* king.

10.

Percy and Bardolph led the way,
But without full control ;
In vain did they the wild men pray
To have one heart and soul.

11.

Small jealousies, with growing greed,
Derang'd the gathering ;
Of rising quarrels, great the need
To hinder the outbreaking.

12.

No easy task for harass'd men
(Accustom'd to command
Devoted followers) now to gain
A moral upper hand.

13.

No easy task to regulate
The license of marauders,
When they began to desolate
England's side of the Borders.

14.

Percy commanded the Foot force,
Lacking that energy
Which Bardolph had to head the Horse
In an emergency.

15.

Percy was old, and sorely shatter'd,
His strength was in despair ;
Bardolph, though toil and travel batter'd,
Still young—able to dare.

16.

High courag'd—rising to the need—
Goaded by Faith and Hope—
And only wanting, to succeed,
An even chance and scope.

17.

The news preceded them to York,
" That they who once did flee
Now brought a Scottish power, to work
Out England's liberty.

22

18.

" Now raised the Standard of Revolt
For the TRUE SOVEREIGN ;
And that in Yorkshire they did halt
To fight for HIM again."

19.

Some ready, loyal partisans
Responded to the call,
But many willing, fear'd the chance
Might still against them fall.

20.

The creatures of the ruthless *king*
Of course took part with him,—
Earl Westmoreland, in marrying
The sister of old " Grim,"

21.

Prov'd worthy of his " Gaunt " ally ;
Sir Thomas Rokeby, too,
The Yorkshire sheriff, " faithfully,"
His " duty " *he* must do (!)

22.

Summon the forces of the shire
Ere men had time to think—
Taking for granted none desire
What he himself would blink.

23.

False to his fallen feudal lord—
Time-serving to his *king*—
He did what best he could *afford*,
Just like every worldling.*

24.

" Away, away with the marauders ! "
Sir Thomas Rokeby said ;
" Percy and Bardolph are intruders,
A price is on their head.

25.

" Their very carrion is gold,
Which all may earn who dare ;
And they who need to be twice told
Shall not the bounty share.

---

* Sir Thomas Rokeby was a vassal of the Earl of Northumberland; and the king rewarded his defection to the earl by one of
the earl's own manors. (See the ensuing note, and that at the end
of Part VIII.)

26.

" Away, away to *Haslewood*,
Away to *Bramham Moor*,*
Drive back the black mail reiving brood,
The plunderers of our poor ! "

27.

So strove the Sheriff to engage
The sympathies of men,
Who car'd not whose war they did wage,
So they might PEACE obtain.

28.

Lord Bardolph also had to plead
And teach a *foreign* power ;
Men unaccustom'd to his lead,
And to his martial lore.

---

* In a small book entitled "The Battles and Battlefields of Yorkshire, by William Grainge," published in 1854, by A. Hall, London, and J. Hunton, York, is the following account :—"The king, hearing of the invasion, and threatened insurrection, quickly assembled a powerful force, and hastened with all speed towards his enemies. Before he could arrive at the scene of action, Sir Thomas Rokeby, sheriff of Yorkshire, assembled the forces of the county to oppose the earl, who was desolating the country as he passed along. In order to interrupt their course, or bring them to battle at a disadvantage, the sheriff took post at Grimbald Bridge, near Knaresborough, on a strong piece of ground, with the river Nidd, flowing between deep and rocky banks, in front, and where a small army would have the advantage of a large one. The earl seeing this, made no attempt to force the passage, and turned aside, and arrived at Wetherby by another route, closely pursued by the sheriff. From Wetherby, the *rebels* turned to Tadcaster, and finally (when they found that they must either fight or fly) to *Bramham Moor*, near *Haslewood*, where the earl chose his ground, drew up his forces, and offered battle to the sheriff, who, on his part, was quite ready to accept it ; and, with the standard of St. George spread, set upon the earl, who fought under a standard of his own arms. From the accounts we have of the battle, it appears to have been contested with great fury, for the time it continued : after "*a sore encounter and cruel conflict, the victory fell to the sheriff.*" The Lord Bardolph was taken prisoner, but so severely wounded that he died shortly afterwards. The Abbot of Hales being taken in arms, was executed at York, with many others of the party. The Bishop of Bangor experienced a milder fate, for, *not* being taken in arms, his life was spared. Northumberland was slain outright, and thus, by an honorable death in the field, escaped the more ignominious fate that had otherwise befallen him. His head, "*full of silver hoary hairs,*" was put upon a stake, then carried through London, and placed upon the Bridge, along with [that] "[one of the quarters]" of Lord Bardolph. " For this piece of service, the king granted to Sir Thomas Rokeby the manor of Spofforth *(formerly belonging to the earl)*, with all its appurtenances, during his life."

29.

But the time press'd—the work begun
(However ill the training)
By some means must be carried on—
'T were bootless now complaining.

30.

Herein was Patience made complete,
In striving against odds!
Herein was he prov'd truly GREAT—
And thus he spoke in words.

31.

" Prepare to fight, my valiant friends,
As you ne'er fought before ;
Fortune—Life—England—All depends
Now upon *Bramham Moor*.

32.

" Knights ! noble knights ! who seek in fights
Of knighthood to make proof,
Drink now the draught that so delights—
GLORY is your behoof.

33.

"If Love and Beauty charm the soul—
If Honor fire the breast—
If Duty should and does control—
Let Valor do the rest.

34.

" Brave cavaliers of each degree,
Heroes and comrades all,
The smaller laws of chivalry
To memory recal.

35.

"Impart your spirit to your steeds,
Arouse their warlike rage ;
In unison do rival deeds,
Soon as we once engage.

36.

" Knuckle the saddle with the knee,
In stirrup sink the heel ;
Shorten the reins, firmly and free
Your horses' mouths to feel.

37.

" Curve the rein-elbow out of harm,
Clear of the sabre sweep ;
On either side, let the right arm
Have reach both long and deep.

38.

"Straighten and strengthen manhood's form,
   And let your manly hearts
Defy the furious battle storm
   When each brave charger starts.

39.

"Keep line and distance well in view,
   Both centre and outsiders;
Forward—and forward! through—and through!
   Then back again, Rankriders!

40.

"The rightful king—we fight for him—
   And if our fight prevails,
With him we gloriously redeem
   A rightful "Prince of Wales."*

41.

"Now then, horsemen, "OPEN THE BALL!"
   Look at yon glorious sun!
This day, before its final fall,
   Must desperate work be done.

42

"You that have wives, strike for your lives!
   Or think of them no more;
Lest orphan childhood you survives,
   Exert your utmost power.

43.

"Should we be beat, there's no retreat—
   No more the hope of "Home!"
Either the victory we get,
   Or else, the world to come!"

*   *   *   *

44.

The armies met—the armies clos'd—
   And, though the Gael fought well,
The Scots by Saxons were oppos'd,
   Whom it takes time to quell.

45.

The Gaul—the Gael—the genial Erse—
   Though lavish of their blood,
Concentred not their common force
   As the cool Saxon could.

---

* Both Edmund Mortimer Earl of March, the rightful heir of
England, and Owen Glendor, *were blood descendants of* LLEWELLYN,
the last reigning Prince of Wales, which neither the *usurper* Henry
IV., nor his son Henry V., could claim to be.

46.

In quick advances and retreats,
    In cunning and in skill,
In marches, feints, and furtive feats,
    The *Gaul* is master still.

47.

In border raids and enterprise,
    As if for hunting meets,
In taking places by surprise,
    The *Gael* the *Saxon* beats.

48.

But in the open battle field,
    Stern struggle, and stern strife,
The Anglo-Saxon hates to yield,
    Except he yield his life.

49.

Bardolph had none of his own troops,
    Grown to his discipline ;
Long since, dispers'd in little groups,
    At home, they hide and pine.

50.

Earl Percy also wish'd in vain
    For soldiers of his mould ;
The tyrant of these outlaw'd men
    Kept them in his own hold.

51.

It is not merely *limbs* we need—
    It is not live *machines* ;
We want the *heart*, we want the *head*,
    We want the *moral* means.

52.

Men of an apt, yet generous stamp,
    As proud to serve as rule,
Whose faith, reverses do not damp,
    In lessons learnt at school.

53.

Men of a simply noble mind,
    With talent to discern
Between the shams that seek to blind
    And real fires that burn.

54.

A man 's a man—do all we can
    To knead him like a cake ;
Though strict to " form and order " plan,
    Still he is wide awake.

55.

One officer he thinks the best,
Another deems the worst ;
One he prefers to all the rest,
Another holds accurst.

56.

One, he will follow in the fight
With promptitude and joy ;
One, he will blight with all his might,
Yet *not seem* to annoy.

57.

How much *more* will he spurn a foe,
How much more mind a chief,
When Love and Duty urge him to
Exertions past belief.

58.

But how much *less* when carelessness
Of all moral restraint—
When sordid fear, or avarice,
The soldier feelings taint.

59.

Men may be demons, may be gods,
And this may all depend
On *Governmental* vice and frauds,
Or on *one* wise *good friend*.*

60.

The foreigners, however brave,
At plunder came to play ;
They car'd not this good land to save,
But for the sterling pay.

---

* The names of " Rowland Lord Hill " and " Sidney Herbert "
will be ever fragrant in the soldier's recollection as the soldier's
friends ; but the actual " Government " treatment of the actual
living, dying, and deceased officers and soldiers of the army of the
late Honourable East India Company—in depriving them *(contrary
to Parliamentary pledge)* of their status, promotions, prospects,
privileges, hard-earned prize-money, and due rewards of their toils,
privations, sufferings, losses, and heroisms, in quelling the disas-
trous Indian Mutiny of 1857-1859 [and, *per contra*, in favoring
and feathering any untried bantling of the Royal army]—is treatment of the most demoralizing character and dangerous tendency,
and such as must preclude the possibility of any more such heroes,
gentlemen, statesmen, and patriots, as Clive, Lawrence, Outram,
and " European soldiers of their mould."

In *Hearts* of *Oak* we glory ; and we should :
But woe betides us when their HEADS are WOOD.

61.

High and heroic sentiments
Were lost upon freebooters ;
Some needed but a slight pretence
To fly from the sharp-shooters.

62.

Expending fury in hot haste
Against the Yorkshire men,
Who stood the onset, as if brac'd
To stand to it again.

63.

They rallied not from their own shock
(Which did not prove effective),
But spent—and breath'd—and order broke,
(With panic fear re-active).

64.

In single-handed desperation,
Some dar'd to stay and fight ;
While others seiz'd on the occasion
Of despair—to take flight.

65.

The well mass'd forces held their way—
And, as a ball that bowls,
Increases in velocity
The more down hill it rolls,

66.

So the unbroken Yorkshire ranks,
Though thinn'd by the first blow,
Quickly supplied their casual blanks
And doubled on their foe.

67.

Faster and faster trod their path,
Fierce to retaliate ;
And, in the vengeance of their wrath,
EARL PERCY met his fate !

68.

LORD BARDOLPH made his charger leap,
While shouting to his train—
" Spur, rowel deep ! line order keep !
Flesh your swords ! fighting men ! "

69.

Firmly he drove the hostile horse—
(Determin'd they should yield)
The dread encounter shook the force,
And many a charger reel'd.

70.

He watch'd the work—they did it well—
" Hurrah ! hurrah ! Rankriders ! "
But the chief praise and honor fell
To those who were outsiders.

71.

His centre waver'd ! from the rear
He speeded to the front ;
Amid the carnage, made a clear--
No danger him could daunt.

72.

" Mountjoy St. Denny ! Mighty George !
Saint Andrew—Patrick—David !
Men of all lands ! TOGETHER CHARGE !
Death summons all to brave it !

73.

" Ride through and through ! " he sternly cried
To those who stood the shock—
" Forward and forward—men of pride—
Hold your own like a rock ! "

74.

The dead—the dying—form'd a heap—
A fence between the foes ;
A stumbling trap, or bar to leap,
Whichever any chose.

75.

Over he flew—onward he fled—
All who oppos'd him fell ;
The brave—the base—alike he sped
To heaven, or to hell.

76.

His gallant bearer bore him on,
Each moment more excited ;
The sabre flying up and down,
His starting eyeballs frighted.

77.

More and more frantic in the course
Of limb and body riving ;
Nor man, nor horse, could stand the force
Of horse and man thus driving.

78.

As to the demon of the storm,
They yielded terror-stricken ;
While those behind— their leader mind,
And their own powers quicken.

23

79.

Bravely they follow'd in his wake,
    Although in broken fashion—
[More dead resistance is a check,
    However wild we dash on.]

80.

His thrilling *word* erewhile had stirr'd
    Each man to do his best ;
But, by his mighty *prowess* spurr'd,
    They fought like men possess'd—

81.

And those who waited on the chief,
    Emerging through the fray—
Resolv'd *with him* to come to grief,
    Or *with him* win the day.

82.

Before them stood the foe's reserve,
    In order of attack ;
One gallop'd up, " the *king* to serve,"
    And drive the baron back.

83.

For fierce collision both prepar'd,
    In fierce collision met ;
Lord Bardolph's head was quickly bar'd,
    St. George's guard not set.

84.

The furious blow his helmet broke,
    And clean cut was the crown ;
Both horses stagger'd with the shock—
    Horses and men went down.

85.

The blow itself not un-return'd,
    For with a rapid eye
And ready hand that quickly learn'd,
    He lung'd a keen reply.

86.

His fate he stak'd upon that *thrust*,
    Forc'd through his enemy,
Who rolling, writhing in the dust,
    Groan'd his last agony.

87.

The baron held his hilt secure,
    And rose with all his might ;
When lo ! the blade was there no more,
    But broke off in the fight !

88.

Though stunn'd, and strain'd, and sharply pain'd,
And shaken with the fall,
He liv'd, and had the vantage gain'd,
Although that might be small. *

89.

He heeded not his cloven helm,
His temples streaming blood,
But, as though victor of the realm,
Undaunted still he stood—

90.

Doubtful whether to soar aloft,
Or yet awhile to stay,
To finish aught before he doff'd
His tenement of clay.

91.

Numbers approach'd him—unarm'd—lost
While he the query makes
Whether to wrest, at any cost,
Some soldier's battle-axe?

92.

In a death gripe and grapple, might
He still a foeman slay;
Yet would he not in such way fight
His ebbing strength away.

---

* The author well remembers an officer of the FIFTEENTH
HUSSARS who had a similar experience at Sahagun, in Spain, on
the 21st December, 1808; when about 700 French horsemen stood
opposed to between 300 and 400 British sabres, by whom the
French were charged and overthrown; and, after some sharp fighting, there were taken prisoners by the FIFTEENERS (besides killed
and wounded) 2 Lieut.-Colonels, 11 other officers, 154 privates,
125 horses, several mules, and a quantity of baggage. The officer
referred to (*Lieutenant* and *Adjutant* Charles Jones), after the
charge, was left on the ground insensible, but upon reviving, discovered that he lay beside a dead French dragoon, in whose body
stuck his own broken blade, and by whose sabre he himself had
been cut down. The writer of this note was, at that time, not yet
six years old, but he clearly remembers being at Portsmouth, with
his parents, at the previous embarkation of the troops; and how
distressed he was when his father's charger " SPOT " (a white mare
with black dots, like a Danish dog) was hoisted into the transport;
and how, having obtained a cord, he tied his father in an arm
chair, lest he also should embark during the night, which he did,
" when the child was asleep "; and *that child* now possesses his
father's medal for that campaign, which ended at Corunna, with
the death of General Sir John Moore.

93.

Why care to take *one* other life
When yielding up his own ?
His orphan *children*, and his *wife*,
He thought of—and knelt down.

94.

" God everlasting! God most good ! "
The sinking warrior sigh'd—
" Bless *them*, and *her* in widowhood—
Take *me !* " and then he died.

95.

True—while a breathing body he
Was carried from the spot ;
True—that the joyous enemy
Could boast a prisoner brought.

96.

True—all the vengeance of the *king*
Might on that victim fall—
On whose one person he would bring
The penalty of all.*

97.

But he escap'd the prison bands,
The manacles and fetters ;
He fled—at the Most High's commands—
From the false king's abettors.

98.

In vain around his form they clos'd,
Each guard relieving guard ;
" At midnight," while they thought he dos'd,
He ceas'd his breathing hard !

---

* Lord Bardolph, it seems, was even more obnoxious to the king's revenge than Earl Percy himself, for, in the criminal charges alleged against them, it is recorded that—" les ditz Henry de Percy et Thomas de Bardolf firent les Escotz, enemys du Roy, entrer la ville (de notre dit Seigneur le Roy) de Berwick, et meme la ville arder ; et que le dit Henry de Percy, *par conseil du dit Thomas de Bardolf*, ordeina, et constitua, par ses lettres patenz desoutz le seal de ses armes, certeins ses ambassadeurs, pur communer, treter, et concorder ovesque le dit Robert, nadgairs Roy d'Escose, et auxi ovec certeins ambassatours de France, en destruccion de notre dit Seigneur le Roy, a leur pouair, et de son Roiaulme d'Engleterre, &c. et que les ditz Henry de Percy et Thomas de Bardolf feurent notoirement adherants et de conseil, et covyn, ovesque les Escotz, et puis ovesques les rebelles en Galles, &c. &c."—(Lib. de Ant. Leg. pref. p. 144.)

99.

By an angelic escort led,
　He mounted off the world ;
Upward—" march orders " he obey'd ;
　Downward—defiance hurl'd !

100.

Upward—his noble spirit soar'd,
　Amid the bright array ;
His own bright pinions spread abroad,
　Eas'd of their load of clay.*

101.

Upward—and upward—through the height,
　" From strength to strength " he springs,
To lay the Reason of his flight
　Before the King of Kings.†

102.

Upward—and upward—still away,
　Until in vision clear
He sees the Everlasting Day
　And his REDEEMER there—

103.

Surrounded by those SHINING ONES,
　All dazzling in snow white,
Who utter the melodious tones
　Of unalloy'd delight.

104.

While their Ten Thousand voices blend,
　He join'd the harmony—
" O LAMB OF GOD ! WORLD WITHOUT END,
　THINE IS THE VICTORY ! " ‡

105.

So died Lord Bardolph! had he liv'd
　And EDMUND come to reign,
WYRMYOEY had *not* been depriv'd—
　A confiscate demesne—

---

* " Though ye have lien among the pots, yet shall ye be as the
wings of a dove, that is covered with silver, and has feathers like
gold."—Psalm lxviii., 13.
† " They go from strength to strength ; every one of them in
Zion appeareth before God."—Psalm lxxxiv., 7.
‡ " And I heard THE VOICE of MANY ANGELS round about the
Throne—TEN THOUSAND TIMES TEN THOUSAND, AND THOUSANDS
OF THOUSANDS !"—Rev., v., 9, &c.

106.

Disparted—and dispers'd—possess'd
By *gentle* men and *holy*—
Who, deeming it a blighted waste,
Deem Duty to it—Folly! *

107.

Its Baron now, though Earl or Duke,
Would, for chief title crave—
" BARDOLPH," who KING, nor FRIEND, forsook—
The TRUE—the GOOD—the BRAVE!

---

* King Edward VI., in his 4th year, 11th April, gave the site
of the *Priory* of Wirmegay, and *Manor*, together with the *Rectory*,
which was appropriated thereto, to *Thomas Thirlby*, Bishop of
Norwich; but *Edmund Scambler*, who was made Bishop of Norwich in the 27th of Elizabeth, and doing (as Sir Henry Spelman
observes) *as much as well he might to impoverish his church*, made
a lease of most of the manors and lands thereof, *and of the nunnery
of Blackborough* adjoining, to Queen Elizabeth, for 80 years, *at the
lowest rent he might ;* which, Bishop Godwin termeth, in like cases,
" SACRILEGE."—(See Blomfield, and Parkin, on Wermegay.)

The following items are extracted from the " Liber de Antiquis Legibus," preface page 118.

" At the battle of Bramham Moor, fought on the 19th February, 1408, Sunday next after the feast of St. Valentine, the Earl of Northumberland was slain, and Lord Bardolph so severely wounded that he expired before the midnight hour had passed, a prisoner in the hands of the victors.

" According to the sentence passed in 1406, the heads of these noblemen were severed from their bodies, and the remaining portions of the headless trunks divided into four parts. On the Close Roll of the 9th year of Henry IV., under the heading " de capitibus et quarteriis Henrici Percy, nuper Comitis Northumbrie, et Domini de Bardolf, super pontem Londiniarum ponendis," we read as follows :—

I.

" Rex Vice-comitibus Londiniarum salutem.

" Precipimus vobis firmiter quod CAPUD Henrici Percy, nuper Comitis Northumbrie, et *unum quarterium* corpori‹ Thome nuper Domini de Bardolf, proditorum nostrorum, cum capud et quarterium illud vobis ex parte nostra liberata fuerint, ea super pontem civitatis predicte modo quo ante hec tempora in hujusmodi casu fieri consuevit poni faciatis.

" Teste Rege apud Westmonasterium x$^{mo.}$ die Marcii per breve de privato sigillo."

II.

" Rex Majori et Ballivis civitatis sue Lincolnie, salutem.

" Precipimus vobis firmiter injungentes, quod CAPUD Thome nuper Domini de Bardolf, et *unum quarterium* corporis Henrici Percy, nuper Comitis Northumbrie, proditorum nostrorum, cum capud et quarterium illud ex parte nostra liberata fuerint, ea in locis civitatis predicte, modo quo ante &c." (ut supra).

The other quarters of the Earl of Northumberland were sent to York, Newcastle-upon-Tyne, and Berwick-upon-Tweed; and those of Lord Bardolf to York, Shrewsbury, and to the town of Lynn, *in the vicinity of his castle of " Wermigey."*

III.

In the month of April of this same regnal year, the king yielded to the request of the widow of Thomas Lord Bardolf, to allow the head and body of her ill-

fated husband to be interred; as we learn from this
entry on the Roll of Letters Patent, headed "de
capite et quarteriis sepeliendis."

"Rex Maiori et Vice-comitibus Londiniarium,
salutem.

"Supplicavit nobis *Avicia*, que fuit uxor *Thome*
nuper Domini de Bardolf, ut eidem *Avicie* capud et
corpus ejusdem *Thome* ad ea in sacra sepultura
sepelienda concedere velimus. Nos, supplicacioni
predicte annuentes, vobis mandamus quod unum
quarterium corporis predicti *Thome* supra pontem
civitatis predicte de mandato nostro nuper positum,
prefate *Avicie*, aut ejus attornato, hoc breve nostrum
vobis deferenti, liberetis sepeliendum in forma predicta. Teste Rege apud Pontefreyt xiii. die Aprilis,
per ipsum regem."

Similar command was sent to the Mayor and
Bailiffs of *Lincoln*, to deliver up the *head* upon the
gate of their city; as also to the Mayor and Bailiffs
of the town of *Lynn*; to the Mayor and Sheriffs of
York; and to the Bailiffs of the king's town of
Shrewsbury, to deliver up the other three quarters
for interment, with the king's "teste" of the same
date.

The head and body of *Henry* Earl of *Northumberland* were also delivered up for interment, pursuant
to similar letters patent, bearing date at Westminster, on the second day of July, in the same year.

WERMIGEY.

PART X.

ON EARTH—IN HEAVEN—AND IN HELL.

" Many Waters cannot quench Love,
    Neither can the Floods drown it—
" For Love is strong as Death,
    Bereavement dreadful as the Grave."
                        SONG OF SOLOMON.

1.

O Death! we should not so much dread
  Thy wintry, watry weather,
If those who in Love's links are wed
  Might always die together.

2.

He is not to be pitied, who
  Lies quiet in his shroud;
But they who lov'd him, and must now
  Round his dead body crowd.

3.

He is not to be pitied, who
  Can never more be sad;
But he, or she, who have to do
  Without the cheer they had.

4.

He is not to be pitied, who
  Has found the way to God;
But they whose hearts are cut in two,
  And cannot see that road.

5.

There may, indeed, for aught we know,
  Be *some* pain in that soul,
Who, though in heaven, leaves below
  One *half* of his own whole.

24

6.

There are *draw-backs* in heaven's bliss!
For God Himself aspires
That man may not His glory miss—
AND MAN BAULKS GOD'S DESIRES!

7.

Angels, we know, are full of woe
When they see souls expire
Who are bound, hand and foot, to go
Into the quenchless fire.*

8.

And when we see our lov'd ones flee
From good ways to the bad,
So likewise we must wretched be
Though all around are glad.

9.

BARDOLPH, no doubt, perceiv'd the lack
Of *her* he so much lov'd;
But wil'd the time in thinking back
The blisses he had prov'd;

10.

And in preparing for the bridal
When they should reunite;
Forestalling joy, and beside all
Praying with his whole might

11.

For her felicity on earth,
So long as that might last,
Before that wonderful New Birth
Which Death is—when Life's past!

*   *   *   *

12.

Speedy the news of the defeat,
And of the "prisoner" made,
The brother, wife and children meet,
And they the *king* waylaid.

13.

The *king* was hastening to the scene,
With forces in support
Of Rokeby—when they came between
And by the mantle caught.

---

* See Matt., iv., 11; Mark, xxii., 13; Luke, xv., 7–10; and
xvi., 22; Heb., xii., 1.

14.
The children—" children " now no more —
Were upgrown in three years ;
[Time, pass'd in learning sorrow's lore,
A century appears.]

15.
The mother offer'd not to sue,
  She only prompted them,
To be to their own nature true
  And stir the *king* to shame.

16.
" Lord king ! for Christ's sake ! spare my sire ! "
  Each trembling daughter cried ;
" Forbear to tempt the Almighty's ire,
  Which no man can abide.

17.
" Restore the parent to the child—
  Hear Innocency plead ;
Or, be with him but reconcil'd,
  And make the children bleed.

18.
" Make us the victims of thy wrath,
  A sacrifice for him ;
If vengeance must find out a path,
  Let *our* lives *his* redeem ! "

19.
The dark Usurper view'd the pair
  As though indeed they ow'd
Their lives as well—and so their prayer
  Was bootlessly bestow'd.

20.
More, rather than *less* angeréd,
  He gave the order—" *Strike !*
*And quickly rear the sever'd head
  Upon a six foot pike !*

21.
" *Nay more : divide the dead remain !
  Disperse it far asunder ;
That York and London—Lincoln—Lynn
  And Shrewsbury folk may wonder !*

22.
" *On each town gate exalt them straight,
  Also on London Bridge ;
Let all who stare and shrink thereat
  Count it a privilege !* "

23.

The sentence dread—not lingeréd—
The mandate was obey'd ;
Thus mangled were the slaughter'd dead—
That penalty they paid!

24.

O Heaven! in this world of ours
The works are works of *Hell!*
And Thou dost not annul its powers,
Being Inscrutable!

25.

Aye—" Wait, wait, wait the after-death,
Aye—" Wait the Judgment Day ;
Aye—" Wait till fleeting human breath
Has stopp'd, and pass'd away ! "

26.

True : but our Life's impulsive blood
Endures no future time ;
Whether for Evil or for Good,
Now—*now*—rings like a rhyme.

27.

Yet "wait " we must, O Sovereign Will!
" Wait " till Thy Day of Doom;
Grow stiller—stiller—and more still—
Until " THY KINGDOM COME ! "

28.

The children and the widow too
Endur'd the loss of all :
Home—Husband—Father—Fortune flew
At the Usurper's call.

29.

The woe-worn widow wearied not
Her duty to perform ;
Her lov'd lord's livid limbs she brought
Together—each place from.

30.

She pray'd her friends to pray the *king*
(Of whom she had a horror)
From shame, not as her pitying,
To grant them to her sorrow.

31.

" O Jesu—Jesu—most unkind !
O cruel—cruel God ! "
[*So thought she in her inner mind,*
Though she spoke not aloud.]

32.

" I had so trusted Thee, in hope
    I might not too much bear—
That Thou wouldst never let me drop
    Down deep into despair.

33.

" Poor victim—of, I know not *what*—
    Nay—of, I know not *whom*—
Is there, indeed, a GOD, or *not ?*
    Is there a World-to-come ? "

34.

The Head and Quarters ! O the pain,
    The torture of her soul !
O the dread joy to get again
    All that could make *him* whole !

35.

O the mad pleasure then to treasure
    Him in a coffin laid ;
Though marr'd and mangled beyond measure,
    " *My husband still !* " she said.

36.

" *My husband !* " though her senses reel'd,
    And stupor veil'd her sight,
As though the truth could be conceal'd
    By shutting out the light !

37.

" *My husband !* was it thus to be
    When, in youth's rosy prime,*
We thought that all things must agree
    To gladden our life-time !

38.

" As *then,* our mutual love and bliss
    Transcended HEAVEN (we thought),
So *now* thy " Sweetheart,"—" Wife,"—" Avice,"
    Down to " THE DEEP " is brought ! †

39.

" Companion—Friend—Pride—Comfort—Life—
    My " Treasure,"—*my* " Cinqfoil ! "
Hell's envy set the world at strife
    Our happiness to spoil.

---

* See part ii., page 35, verse 69.
† " De profundis clamavi."—Psalm cxxx., 1.

40.

" And He, who had ordain'd our lot,
  Could be so far unkind—
(Though we His tender mercy sought)
  To fling it to the wind! "

41.

Thus, at one while, would she beguile,
  Yet aggravate despair ;
Her woes heap up—pile upon pile—
  Then melt away in prayer.

42.

" Eternal Being ! come and take
  The breath which thou hast breath'd !
Quench, or else quicken, for Christ's sake,
  My soul—in sorrow seeth'd.

43.

" As, when in childhood, on my brow
  A Diamond Coronet,
So, on that brow, my Saviour, now,
  Thy Crown of Thorns is set !

44.

" For ever ? not for ever thus
  Can I Thy Passion bear ;
Thou didst not suffer—me to curse—
  But Paradise to share.

45.

" As Thou wast pierc'd and agoniz'd,
  And Thy Form crucified,
So am I now by Thee chastis'd,
  To be more glorified.

46.

" Is it not so ? I know it is,
  Else Thou wouldst be untrue ;
Thy Jewels, bought at bloody price,
  Thou wilt have bloody too ! *

47.

" *Five* wounds *Thee* gor'd, Thou sacred Lord,
  And *he* is cut asunder ;
In those FIVE MORSELS which I hoard
  Until Thy Judgment's Thunder.

---

* The Jewels of Jehovah ?—See Malachi, iii., 17.

48.

" Have Mercy! only hold me up
  Until Thou canst receive ;
If I *must* drink and drain this cup,
  Oh ! may I still believe

49.

" That, freed from guilt, by Thy Blood spilt,
  He shall again be *mine ;*
And, at our " House in Heaven " built,
  My Spouse I shall rejoin ! " *

50.

So, the once happy, peerless dame,
  True wife—true widow—tried
To emulate God's Holy Lamb
  In all she said and did.

51.

Her sorrows did not turn her brain,
  But, by a strange caprice,
She would not let the " arms " remain
  As in the old device.

52.

Instead of three, *five* cinqfoils she
  Insisted should adorn
The BARDOLPH equipage, and be
  Throughout her livery worn.†

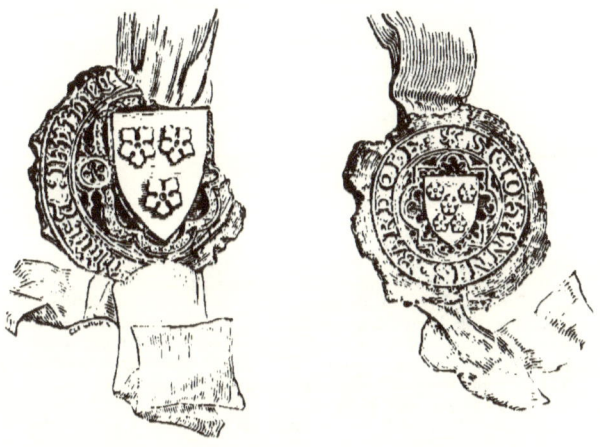

---

* See 2 Peter, i., 4 ; and 2 Cor., v., 1– 2 ; and John, xiv., 2.
  † See the Bardolph seals in the Notes to Part II.

53.

Five—number five—she would contrive
To count in every thing ;
Stars—flowers—senses—features—strive
To rule by *finger*-ing.*

54.

Five parcels, in a coffin laid,
Seem'd ever on her mind ;
And " the right number," (so she said)
" Must ever be combin'd ! "

55.

Oh ! beautiful is True Love's grief,
As beautiful its joy ;
Reason may wreck, through unbelief,
But Love floats like a buoy !

56.

Love shall o'erride the Wrecks of Time
Until the sea be dry ; †
True Faith—true Hope—may help us *climb*,
But True Love storms the sky ! ‡

57.

The loving, lovely Avice-Ann,
Though in her bloom of life,
Endur'd no offer to enchain
Her as another's wife.

58.

A halo of religious awe
Her presence did invest,
Forcing respect from Power and Law
And sordid Interest.

---

* " It is related of Isabella de Fortibus, Countess of Aumale and
Devon, and Lady of the Isle of Wight (which she granted, with
other manors, to King Edward I.), that, on the day she made her
will, she named, *by her fingers*, her executors ; namely, the Abbot
of Quarr—the Prior of Bremmore—the Prior of Christ Church—
and Gilbert de Knevill ; and being thereby fatigued, she retired to
rest ; and after having partaken of the Holy Communion, at the
hands of her confessor (Brother William of Gainsburgh), between
midnight and dawn, 12 Nov. (23 Edward I.) she expired."—(See
Lib. de Leg. Ant. pref. p. ex.)

† " And there shall be no more sea ! "—Rev., xxi., 1 ; and
xxii., 3.

‡ " The kingdom of heaven suffereth violence, and the violent
take by force."—Matt., xi , 12.

59.

There are *no second* marriages—
Or else, there are *no first ;*
Or, both are dream-like bev'rages
That slake not the soul's thirst :—

60.

Profanities, or parodies—
Like figures drawn in dust—
Or water-rippled *mimicries*
Of one grand classic bust !

61.

We are not born with many hearts,
  We can have only one ;
And one we cannot give in parts,
  We must give all or none.

62.

When True Love truly fills the breast
  With one whom we adore,
That one is First, that one is Last,
  There is no room for more.*

63.

As well may we have *many* gods,
  And the One God blaspheme ;
Or seek that God by *devious* roads,
  As of two True Loves dream.†

64.

The Lady Avice and her lord,
  Angelically sprung,
Drew their love-knot in one firm cord,
  To one fast anchor strung.

65.

A better barony above
  Endows that noble pair ;
The Love of Truth—the Truth of Love
  None can take from them there.

---

* " Did He not at the Beginning make them One ? And wherefore One ? that they might have GODLY CHILDREN."—(See Malachi, ii., 15 ; and Matt., xix., 4—8).

† "There is one God—and one Mediator between God and man,
the Man Christ Jesus—and there is none other name under Heaven, whereby we can be saved, but only the name of Jesus—the
same yesterday, to-day, and for ever !"—(See 1 Tim., ii., 5 ; and
Acts, iv., 12 ; and Heb., xiii., 8.)

66.

God made them one—and they are one,
Impossible to sever;
In one rapt kiss of deathless bliss
Their souls are seal'd for ever! *

67.

In heaven, that holy happy tie
Is not as upon earth; †
They do not marry doubtingly,
Or think of money's worth.

68.

Although an action free will,
There is no selfish choice;
The Bride and Bridegroom only feel
Joy to obey God's voice. ‡

69.

Wearing one crown, they both bow down
And both rise up together;
Crown'd with HIS BLESSING, they can own
Duty—light as a feather.

70.

Wherever order'd to proceed,
Exultingly they go;
Each by the other shadowéd,
As fond young children do. §

---

* "*Aricia*, Lady Bardolph, was deceased on the first day of
July, 1421, in the ninth year of Henry V., having survived her ill-
fated husband 13 years. Wherefore, pursuant to a writ with the
teste of John Duke of Bedford, Guardian of England, at Westminster, 1st October following, an inquisition was taken before
William de Lexam, the escheator of Norfolk and Suffolk, at Bungay, in the last named county, on Tuesday, the feast of the Apostles
St. Simon and St. Jude, 28th October, 1421, which describes her
to have died seized of the manor in Ilketishale, called *Bardolfe's
Hall*, held of the king in chief, by the service of half a knight's fee,
and other tenements in the same vill, called Mendham Fee, held of
the Earl Marshall, John de Mowbray, and embodies this finding of
the jurors, as to her heirs: " Dicunt quod predicta *Aricia* obiit
primo die Julii ultimo preterito, et quod *Anna* (nuper uxor Willelmi
Clifford militis defuncti), et *Joanna* (nunc uxor Willelmi Phelip
militis) filie predicte Avicie, sunt heredes ejusdem Aricie propin-
quiores."— (See Lib. de Leg. Ant. pref. p. 155.)

† "In heaven they neither marry, nor are given in marriage."
(as upon earth) "but are as the angels," "sons and daughters of
the Lord Almighty."—(Matt., xxii., 30 ; and Mark, xii., 25 ; and
Luke, xx., 36 ; and 2 Cor., vi., 18.)

‡ "The Bride the Lamb's wife."—Rev., xxi., 9.)

§ "The Spirit and the Bride say—Come !"—(Rev., xxii., 17.)

71.
'Tis only a new ecstasy,
Whate'er they undertake ;
Priz'd more and more increasingly
After the earth's heart-ache.*

72.
O how they prize each other's faith,
The Husband and the Wife !
O how they breathe each other's breath,
And drink each other's life !

73.
O how their sighing spirits sing
The fulness of their joy !
O how they feed, like lambs in spring,
On fruits which never cloy ! †

74.
Not, as in mirrors down below,
Do they themselves admire ;
But at each other they look so, ‡
And never never tire.

75.
Fresh gleams of beauty they perceive,
Awaking fresh delight ;
They love—and love—and yet believe
They never yet lov'd quite.

76.
And let them love, and happy be,
And evermore rejoice ;
No more to see earth's VILLANY
Or hear a TYRANT'S voice !

*   *   *   *

---

* " Eye hath not seen, nor ear heard, nor heart conceived, what
God hath prepared for them that love Him."—(Isaiah, lxiv., 4 ;
and 1 Cor., ii., 9.
† " Then shall the " [LAMB'S] " *lambs* feed after their manner."
—(Isaiah, v., 17.)
‡ " Moses was admonished of God to make all things in the
Tabernacle *according to the pattern of heavenly things* showed him
in the Mount, &c."—(Heb., viii., 5.) —" One cherub on one end of
the Mercy Seat, and the other cherub on the other, *covering* the
Mercy Seat with their wings, and *their faces looking one to another*
—toward the Mercy Seat."—(Exod., xxv., 17—22.)

77.

Too late, the Fourth King Henry griev'd
The crime-cost of his throne ;
Too late, he sought to be reliev'd
By *merits* to be done.

78.

In vain he built a chapel where
He quarter'd Hotspur's corse,
That priests might offer daily prayer
For all that slaughter'd force

79.

Both on his own and Hotspur's side.
His *crown* became his *cross !*
He saw it on his son's head tried
*While dying of remorse.**

80.

Too often *pious* parents groan
O'er children's selfishness ;
Why should not, then, the *wicked* moan
When theirs give them no peace ?

81.

WHY SHOULD NOT DREAMS OF THWARTED SCHEMES
DISTURB THEIR MORTAL SLEEP
WHO SPAR'D NO PAINS TO GET EARTH'S GAINS
HEEDLESS WHOM THEY MADE WEEP ?

82.

Go, monster ! feed upon the fruits
Of the seeds thou hast sown ;
The Tree of Evil's tangled roots
In thy soul's soil have grown—

---

* The historian *Speed* thus notices this fact : " The vulgar
chroniclers tell us a strange story, the truth of which must rest on
the reporters. The king (say they) lying dangerously sick, caused
his crown to be set on a pillow at his head, when suddenly the
pains of his apoplexy seizing on him so vehemently that all supposed him dead—the prince, coming in, took away the crown,—
which his father, reviving soon after, missed ; and calling for his
son, demanded what he meant by bereaving him of that to which
he had yet no right ? &c."—*Shakespeare* also, in the second part of
his Henry IV., scene iv., thus words the *king's* displeasure :—

" *King Henry*—But wherefore did he take away the crown ?"—
                                 " O foolish youth !
" Thy life did manifest thou lov'dst me not—
" And thou wilt have me die assur'd of it."

83.

Snake-like, but solid, firm and fast,
  Divergent under ground;
Tempests of terror thee may blast,
  But they spread wide around—

84.

No tooth is tighter in thy jaw,
  To *stir* which is a pang;
There is no dentist that can draw
  Remorse's dogged fang.

85.

Go, monster! leave thy stolen throne,
  Thy bauble of a crown;
In hell, go seek what is thine own,
  Boast THERE of thy renown!

86.

Go, bathe in lambent fires, that lick
  Damn'd souls like lighted spears;
For *music*, hear the wretched shriek;
  For *wine*, drink widow's tears.

87.

Count all the *orphans* thou hast made,
  (O what a goodly show!)
How many *bodies without head!*
  (O what a pleasant view!)

88.

How many *faces* ghastly white,
  Distorted in all ways,
But *without bodies?* (splendid sight!)
  Who can deny thy praise?

89.

Go then, and revel—kingly devil!
  Reckon up thy choice treasure;
Thou wilt find others of thy level,
  Who in such things take pleasure;

90.

Those who chew bitter things, like rue,
  And sour things, like sorrel;
And having not enough to do,
  Still with each other quarrel.

91.

Such company is to thy taste,
  So take thy belly-full;
Set to, in Red hot, Royal haste,
  In hell, no things may cool!

* * * *

92.

On these things, let the curtain fall,
  God wishes none to die ;
But deaf are all to hear His call—
  WHO DIE ETERNALLY!

93.

He cannot make Himself aggriev'd
  If men will none of Him ;
If He is not to be believ'd,
  He cannot them redeem.

94.

LIKE SEEKS ITS LIKE—IT CONTRAST SHUNS
  THROUGHOUT THE UNIVERSE ;
The DAY and NIGHT come on BY TURNS,
  THEY CANNOT BOTH CONVERSE.

95.

Like Him—(He knows)—I wish *my* foes
  No suffering, no sore ;
Only that those who made my woes
  May cross my path no more.

96.

No after Ruth revokes a Truth—
  No grief blots out the Past ;
The sins and follies of our youth
  To latest ages last.

97.

There is, indeed, a Sacred Flood
  Able to cancel Fate ;
But hands imbrued in crime and blood
  Prize that, alas ! *too late !*

98.

" TOO LATE—TOO LATE—TOO LATE—TOO LATE ! "
  Lost souls for ever yell ;
" *Too late—too late—too late—too late !* "
  Eternal echoes tell !

*   *   *   *

99.

BARDOLPH is Baron now no more
  Of Castle-Wermigey ;
From dungeon floor to turret tower
  The tyrant's wrath you see.

100.

CASTLE and Castle Guard are gone !
Flags—feathers—cavalcade
No more rejoice the " Westbrig " Down
    At cavalry parade !

101.

Yearly the farmer ploughs that ROAD
    So long the Line of March
From the " Westbrig " Hill Guard's abode
    Down to the West Port Arch.

102.

The OUTER DIKE—that Upland Fence—
    That chain of *Trous-de-loup*—
(The first check to a foe's advance)
    All *that* is fill'd up now !

103.

No tempting leap was that, I trow—
    (It was not made to please)
The boldest rider shouted " Woh !
    " *Gare ! les chevaux-de-frize !* "

104.

The GUILDHALL square—the TOWN so fair—
    Where the drum daily roll'd ;
And the Reliefs won'd to repair
    Ere mounting the Strong-Hold—

105.

When each trim knight, in armor dight,*
    With colors " gold and blue,"
(Shining so bright in the sun-light,
    You scarce could bear the view)

106.

Did, at the Gate, the Baron wait
    To make the Grand Salute,
When all in state with his Fair Mate
    He liv'd in such repute—

107.

When bugle call o'er that fine Hall
    Sang loud, and clear, and sweet,
Whether for ball or festival,
    Reveillée or " Retreat"—

108.

All—all are vanish'd from the spot
    Where these gay glories glow'd ;
The landmarks are almost forgot,
    All now is so down trod.

────────────

* deckt.

109.

The very WATERS now are dried
Off the denuded fen,
Which only a sea driving tide
Recovers now and then.

110.

The STONES which form'd the MARKET CROSS
Still lie about the place;
But as to caring for their loss
No man has sense or grace.

111.

The CHURCH, where ancient mourners wept
Their sorrows and their sins,
And where Christ's holy ones have kept
The Feast He still enjoins—

112.

That ancient pile—now so bereft—
So lonely and abhorr'd,
That it, through sacrilegious theft,
Cannot ONE priest afford.*

---

* Both the Prior of Wermigey and his canons, and the Rector of Westbrig and his curate-vicars, are now represented by "one priest" *only*, who is called the perpetual curate of Wermigey and Tottenhill. And these two parishes together *only* supply, out of their own 4238 acres of land—(£12 the one parish, and £20 the other parish, that is, in all) *thirty-two pounds a year* for his maintenance, and *no church-rate*, nor *any other funds*, either for the Holy Houses, or the Holy Offices thereof! Even "God's Acre" (the churchyard) has been purloined from him, and let, and under-let to *traders*, although of late recovered by such energetic measures on his part as ought not to have been needed, and on such conditions as ought not to have been proposed! If, then, the church guardians could so treat any church and parish, is it surprising either that the priest should *vanish*, or that the people should become *pagan?* for such has been the case. However, in the year 1838, a wealthy and worthy scion of the House of *Gournai* (Daniel Gurney, Esq., of North Runcton, Lynn,) put forth a noble effort to reclaim the population from their uncivilized condition, by building a National *school*, projecting a new *church*, and inviting a Welsh *clergyman*, to reside where no English gentleman would advisedly locate himself, especially without adequate and reasonable support. But, after "six weeks' trial," the Welsh clergyman decided that he could not stay; and, after two years, resigned his post to a successor, who has endured the *purgatory*, in his stead, not only of the hostile forces of Romanism, Ranterism, Ruffianism, Highlifed slight, and Lowlifed spight, but also of the still more mean and monstrous "proceedings" of *episcopal* prosecution (in that atrocious relic of the Inquisition, the *so-called* "Ecclesiastical Court of Arches,") *on a false plea*, which happily evoked the loudly spoken sympathy of clergymen who did not live within the diocese of Norwich!

113.

Though once the honor'd, hallow'd shrine
Of " Michael the Great Prince,"
Who stands before the Throne Divine
To plead for human sins.*

114.

That church is in a wilderness,
It shuns the light of day;
And they who witness the distress,
Think scorn the while they pray.†

115.

The Priory! alas! 't was there—
But, like the Bardolph bones,
Divided, scatter'd in the air,
Are its once precious stones.‡

116.

Disguis'd—disfigur'd—and disgrac'd—
The walls down—the site bare—
The very plan is so defac'd,
You scarce believe they *were*.

117.

Some few remains, if well you search,
Pervade the neighbourhood,
Of PILLAR—CAPITAL—or ARCH,
Ill priz'd or understood—

118.

Some flooring TILE of antique style,
Bedeck'd with *fleurs-de-lis*—
And Bardolph's well belov'd *cinqfoil*,
You still may chance to see—

---

* " Michael, the Great Prince, who standeth up for the children of thy people."—Daniel, xii., 1.

† Any thing more sad and secluded than Wermigey church (which is a mile from the village) could scarcely be contrived. The Globe Land, adjoining the churchyard, having been *exchanged* for some distant land, and planted with *trees*, (to prevent reclamation!) these trees completely hide the church on the three sunny sides, so that the churchyard, which is also become a rabbit warren, affords a gloom so blank, and a grass so rank, that the curate's horse, on Sunday during service, will not stay, but stray if he can, because, as the parish clerk (who has so often had to catch him) says, " he downright hates to be there."

‡ That is, built up in barns, cottages, stables, &c.

119.

A VASE, or jug, from fish-pond dug,
Lost centuries ago,
When some poor monk, with his dry hunk,
To fish the ponds would go.*

120.

Although in mode so quaint and rude,
(In works of mercy clever)
It oft o'er-flow'd to do that good
Which God rewards for ever.†

121.

The HOLY FONT, where each young heir
His Christian title got,
Lo! you may find that (I know where)
A garden flower-pot!

122.

THUS TREATED ARE OUR DEAREST TIES,
OUR TENDEREST AFFECTIONS ;
OUR CHARITIES—OUR PIETIES—
OUR VERY NOBLEST ACTIONS !

123.

The " world " is hollow—heartless—mean—
Dull—senseless—commonplace;
The rich who grasp, the poor who glean,
Care not how they deface.‡

---

* Wermigey Priory stood in a close of high ground, within a square moat comprising five acres. And these precincts were surrounded, on one side by its park, (still called " Bushy Field,") and on the others by numerous lakes, or fish-ponds, and farm lands of about 300 acres. The Priory stood north of the Castle about six furlongs, and on the other side of the river which supplied both their moats, and is itself fed by the Marham springs, being quite distinct from the Eye, or Nar, before their junction near Setch, on their way to Lynn. But, in ancient time, the previous overflow of their two currents formed the Great Isle, or "Weir amid the Water."

† " Whosoever shall give to drink a cup of cold water only *for Christ's sake*, shall in no wise lose his reward."—Matthew, x., 42 ; and Mark, ix., 41.

‡ " The world was made by Him, yet the world knew Him not." —John, i., 10. " Whom the world cannot receive."—John, xiv., 17. " Of whom the world was not worthy."—Hebrews, xi., 38. " The Love of God is not in it."—1 John, ii., 15 ; and James, iv., 4.

124.

"The Dogs of War" we hear no more
In *civil* discord yell,
But modern "Vipers of the Law"
Still league our Land with Hell.*

125.

But though the "world" thus mar and mix
Things sacred with profane,
Let CHRISTIANS kiss the CRUCIFIX!
It shall not be in vain.

126.

There is a Treasury on High,
There is a Treasur-ER,
Who hears each brokenhearted sigh,
Who watches every tear.

127.

St. Mary of the Holy Cross!
St. John, the lov'd divine!
And you—who count earth's gain but loss—
Canons of Augustine! †

128.

Where are ye gone? where would ye go?
Not underneath the sod!
You mind not now these things below,
BECAUSE YOU ARE WITH GOD!

129.

O Lifetime! Glory! Goods of Earth!
What fleeting things ye be!
Your homes, your friends, your griefs, your mirth,
Ye DEAD! come back, and see!

* * * *

---

* Without exemplifying the growth of vulgar devilry through
heartless money greed evinced in multifarious law courts—without
offending decency by more than naming that new institution, the
Divorce Court,—the recently repeated TRIALS, in each of the three
kingdoms, to set aside a *true*, an *honest*, and a too *well-deserving*
wife, in favor of her *bigamist* but "honorable" husband (?)—alone
uproot all faith in modern equity and honor, even in the highest
LAW COURTS of the world.

† "The Priory of Wermigey was of the Order of *Augustine* for
Black Canons, and dedicated to the *Virgin Mary*, the *Holy Cross*
and *St. John* the Evangelist.—See Part I., Motto; and Part VI.,
page 125, Note.

CONCLUSION.

" A still small voice " from the departed.

My Spirit was a Ray
  From the Divine One shot !
Through Life's too stormy day
  It found no resting spot,
Till quench'd in a mere flood
  Of ever-welling Tears,
It made escape to God,
  Where the Ray re-appears —
EARTH and its HORRORS to FORGET —
In His Bright Diadem re-set !

Henslowe.

NOTE TO PART X.

Concerning the two daughters of the last " Bardolph" Lord Bardolph.

The two young daughters of the unfortunate Thomas Lord Bardolph were married, it appears, prior to his decease in February, 1408; not only, it is apprehended, *without* his will and consent, but (as part of his confiscated property) in the interest of the usurper.

1. *Anna*, at the age of nineteen, was become the wife of Sir William Clifford, knight ; and

2. *Joanna*, at the age of eighteen, was become the wife of Sir William Phelip, knight.

Sir William Clifford was the second son of Roger Lord Clifford, of Westmoreland, younger brother of Thomas Lord Clifford, and had been Earl Percy's Lieutenant-Governor of *Alnwick Castle*, which he *surrendered* to the king (Henry IV.) after the flight of Earl Percy into Scotland, as also of *Berwick*, and *Fastcastle* in Wales, on behalf of the same Earl and his son Henry Percy.

In the 4th year of Henry V. (1417) he was constable of Bordeaux, but was deceased, without issue, on Friday, the Feast of the Annunciation, 25th March, 1418. His widow, the Lady Anna Bardolph-Clifford, married secondly Sir Reginald Cobham, knight ; but died without issue of either marriage.

Sir William Phelip, the husband of Joanna Bardolph, was the eldest son of Sir William (miscalled by *Dugdale* Sir John), and elder brother of Sir John Phelip, a soldier of distinction, of Donington, Dennington, or Denyngham, in Suffolk. He was born in the year 1383, and became Treasurer of the Household, and also Chamberlain to King Henry V., whom he attended in the wars of France, and had the chief conduct of that king's funeral. He was at the battle of Agincourt, with 8 Lances, and 29 Archers (see page 90, Part V., verse 26, note), and was made a Knight of the Garter, and created " *Lord Bardolph.*" By his will, dated 1st December, 1438, he was buried in the churchyard of St. Margaret, in Donynton, or Denyngham, where he founded a Chantry for two priests, and he died in 19th year of Henry VI.

The annexed three wood engravings represent—

1. The Arms or Shield of Clifford ;
2. The Arms or Shield of Phelip ; and
3. The Monument, or Tomb, in Donyngton church.

of Sir William Phelip, *Lord Bardolph*, and his wife,

NOTE TO PART X.

Joanna Bardolph-Phelip, *Lady Bardolph*. As a pattern of the *military* and *female* costume of the 15th century, a more beautiful monumental specimen is not known to exist.

The shield of Clifford, chequy, *or* and *azure*, a fess *gules*.

The shield of Phelip, quarterly *gules* and *argent*, in first and fourth quarter an eagle displayed *or*.

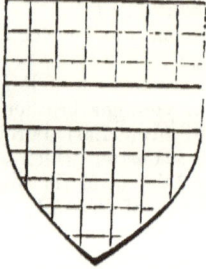 

Monument of Sir William Phelip, "Lord Bardolph," and his wife Joanna Bardolph-Phelip, LADY BARDOLPH.

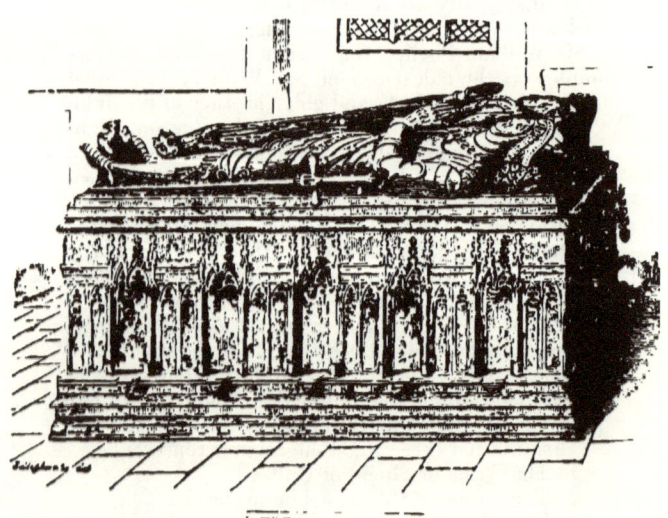

END.

CORRIGENDA.

No.	Page.	Note or verse.	
1.	11.	1. *for* near old Lynn *read* old Lynn near.
2.	13.	21. *for* days *read* day.
3.	14.	29. *for* looked *read* look'd.
4.	15.	32. *for* to the *read* to.
5.	26.	note *for* Cohesey *read* Cokesey.
6.	31.	36. *for* at heart *read* of heart.
7.	34.	64. *for* revered *read* rever'd.
8.	38.	99. *for* care *read* love.
9.	39.	107. *for* surely *read* sorely.
10.	40.	119. *for* interlink't *read* interlinkt.
11.	48.	note on Flag, *for* A.D. 1334 *read* A.D. 1304.
12.	77.	26. *for* bands *read* band.
13.		note. line 12. *for* was slain *read* were slain.
14.	79.	37. *for* might *read* could.
15.	82.	68. *for* avoid his fate *read* avoid fate.
16.	102.	68. *for* belongs *read* belong'd.
17.	105.	96. *for* free *read* own.
18.	105.	98. *for* They were thus *read* Were they.
19.	121.	52. *for* No so *read* Not so.
20.	139.	†. *for* 85-86 *read* 35-36.
21.	152.	5. *for* And so lasted *read* And so long lasted.
22.	160.	63. *for* place *read* pleasure.
23.	—.	66. *for* would *read* could.
24.	165.	99. *for* That which *read* That what.
25.	166.	* (in last line but one) *for* tho forces *read* the
26.	173.	44. *for* glorious *read* soaring.　　　　[forces.
27.	177.	76. *for* sabre *read* faulchion.
28.	—.	77. *for* stand *read* stem.
29.	184.	(fourth line) *for* Londiniarium *read* Londiniarum.